# AFTER
## THE
# BALL
## WAS
# OVER

## ALSO BY ROSEMARY KINGSLAND

A SAINT AMONG SAVAGES

*FOR CHILDREN*

TREASURE ISLANDS

# AFTER
## THE
# BALL
## WAS
# OVER

**Rosemary
Kingsland**

**VIKING**

VIKING

Viking Penguin Inc., 40 West 23rd Street,
New York, New York 10010, U.S.A.
Penguin Books Ltd, Harmondsworth,
Middlesex, England
Penguin Books Australia Ltd, Ringwood,
Victoria, Australia
Penguin Books Canada Limited, 2801 John Street,
Markham, Ontario, Canada L3R 1B4
Penguin Books (N.Z.) Ltd, 182–190 Wairau Road,
Auckland 10, New Zealand

First published in 1985 by Viking Penguin Inc.
Published simultaneously in Canada

LIBRARY OF CONGRESS CATALOGING IN PUBLICATION DATA
Kingsland, Rosemary, 1941–
After the ball was over.
I. Title.
PR6061.I4937A3   1985      823'.914      85-5389
ISBN 0-670-80633-1

Excerpt from "Dancing with Tears in My Eyes" by Joe Burke
and Al Dubin. © 1930 (Renewed) Warner Bros. Inc.
All rights reserved. Used by permission.

Printed in the United States of America by
R. R. Donnelley & Sons Company, Harrisonburg, Virginia
Set in Palatino
Designed by Kathryn Parise

C 0443

*With love and gratitude to my mother,*
ANNIE JOSEPHINE LOTT—
*who survived*

# Jamalpur, India
# 1930

J.M.P., as the small township was called, was a railway station on the East Indian Railway Loopline. It was the workshop for maintaining the rolling stock of the entire E.I.R. Covering a good fifty square miles of flat land in the middle of a purple plain, it grew each year, sprawling aimlessly like a jelly fungus.

J.M.P. was also the training ground for Railway personnel, both official lower class, and the worker, graded according to sports ability, colour, caste, and education, in that order. The real quality bosses were the covenanted, straight out from Blighty wallahs; worshipped, feared, and greatly envied. Every mother with daughters prayed nightly on the cool stone of her bungalow floor: "God send a single man to this heathen place.... Make him covenanted with a large gratuity ... Blighty leaves ... and white—very white."

The town was split into two halves, divided more or less equally by the Railway line. The north side contained Railway workers: white covenanted official, white covenanted unofficial, near-white, and off-white. The south side was the bazaar; police lines; coolie lines; and sprawling, no-good, don't-look-at-'em daughters non-Railway non-Army civil types. All off-white, never-get-to-Blighty mixtures.

The north side was split by a line of shops into private houses and Railway houses. The Railway, since the good

3

days of Queen Victoria, was very royal. Every road paid respect to the great white Empress by bearing first her names—of which she had several—and then those of her large and vigorous family. A stately marble statue of Her Majesty dominated the center of Railway land, maintaining the balance between the favoured on her right hand and the less favoured on her left hand. Her face pointed to the Church of England, the grassy, parklike Maidan (where everyone paraded in the cool of the evening), the reservoir, and the bleak, blue-black range of hills known as the Seven Sisters, which encircled the town and cut it off from the rest of the world. By some freak of nature, Victoria's face, weather-beaten, haughty, had been replicated on one of the crags, and the image carved in volcanic rock and the image carved in white marble matched stare for stare.

The dark, volcanic profile gazed through its pale reflection, looking cruelly upon the Railway yard, the Railway stores-cum-pub, and the Railway Station itself, where every new arrival felt the coldness of her sneer, and not knowing why, shivered apprehensively.

The marble Queen's large left toe (peeping coyly nude from beneath her elaborate robes) pointed to the Institute. Aah! The wind sighed softly through the deodars at the name! The Institute, palace of pleasure for all the acceptable inhabitants. The centre of their universe. Dance, flirt, tipple (Booth's gin, Rawlings' Indian tonic water, and a slice of fresh lime), play bridge or whist, shout housey-housey, Bingo! Clack knitting, clack tongues, slap riding breeches, avoid showing too much silk-stockinged thigh while twirling strings of pearls. Crimp Marcel waves and smile brightly.

But the right toe, plump and sensual—it was where the glistening right toe pointed that was so beloved of all the off-white and near-white unattached females in Jamalpur. A low, rambling collection of buildings, space for a thousand young men, the Apprentices' Hostel, for near-white, non-officer class. Relatively low in status the apprentices might be—*now*—but were they not Railway, permanent, and bach-elors? Were they not assured of good jobs, good Railway houses, and gratuities on retirement? Yes, the apprentices were certainly worth having. One could save on Railway pay and maybe achieve the impossible: retirement in England. And surely, on the way, the sea air would somehow rend a magical change and one would arrive white, so very white (praise the Lord!), chee-chee accent gone, ah yes, ma deah. Land of Hope and Glory!

If one continued in the direction of the pointing toe, past the Apprentices' Hostel, past the compound of lawns, Technical College, workshops, and shady trees, and followed the Grand Trunk Road a mile or so out of town towards Moughyr, one could see the gleaming marble domes of the Maharajah's palace and one could almost smell the great grey ceremonial elephants, hear the trampling of the lordly Arab stallions in the stables, hear the scream of the peacock, hear the song of the bulbul as they swung from purple bougainvillaea and flashed scarlet through the groves of luscious fruits: nectarines, peaches, apricots. The Maharajah, plump, benevolent, had gone to Oxford University in England when he was young and charming, and had enjoyed three giddy strawberry summers on the Thames with a bevy of sweet young things; now his only son was at Eton, learning how to play the game.

The Maidan lay beyond the church. It was a flat green (depending on the weather) expanse, devoid of trees, and lunged out of the town as if attempting to escape to the hills. In some parts of the world it would be considered the town's park, but here it possessed an ambiguous quality, not park, not countryside, not meadow. It was more or less constrained from flight by the encircling embrace of Consort Road, a red mud road most pleasantly shaded by neem trees, cork trees, and tamarinds. The Vicarage lay on the right of the Maidan; then there was a waste of tangled masses of deadly nightshade, datura, and thorny gum arabic. One did not know if the neo-Gothic residence of the man of God was holding the dark poisons at bay, or if the heathen spirits were creeping closer in such a disguise. Certainly the ungodly devils dared not cross the road to opposite the Vicarage, where, screened from curious, irreverent, lustful eyes by a veritable forest of trees, was the Zenana Mission, run by three very English, very memsahibish, very virgin ladies.

The reservoir, the one beauty spot and a favourite lovers' walk, nudged the nightshade wasteland. It was a place where a fisherman, in the damp, reedy smell, could dream of willowed reaches back home in dear old Blighty. Indeed, just beyond the reservoir was a symmetrical, rounded hill, atop of which, peeping through the trees, was a grey castle. This was the pumping station, a folly designed by the Victorian empire-builders who had brought the Railway and the image of their great white Queen.

Beyond the reservoir was the rifle range, exclusively for the use of both the visiting British regiment, whose camp of khaki tents set aflutter every spinster's heart and hopes— "Bless 'em all . . . Bless 'em all . . . the long and the short and the tall . . ."—and the less romantic East Indian Volunteer Regiment, who, like the poor, were always with them; ticks on the lion's back.

Slap bang on the side of the church was an enormous house, a baron's house, with sweeping drives and tended flower-gardens in which weeds wilted with fear and begonias dared not take less than first prize in the Institute flower show. This rococo wonder was the home of the reigning big boss of the J.M.P. Railway Station, Railway Lines, offices, workshops, hostels, and all human souls, brown, white, and off-white. This was the domain of the Controller, the Very Honourable Bertram Papworth, a large, purple-faced, got-a-nasty-smell-under-my-nose, don't-see-anybody-round-here-worth-my-notice type of gentleman.

Next, discreetly knowing their place, came two smaller, less grand houses, belonging to Mr. Nightingale, the Railway Accountant, and Mr. Grundy, Principal of the Railway Apprentices' Technical College. Running past these three houses was the King's Road. Opposite, and separated from the seats of the mighty by high walls and trees, was the Apprentices' (Special Grade, whites only) Hostel and two sprawling, privately owned houses, "The Nest" and "The

Cedars," the latter (owned by Mr. Edwards, businessman, pillar of society, and church elder) named with some degree of hopefulness after the sorry-looking deodars that guarded the iron gates—pretentious iron gates designed as copies of the very gates that guarded Mr. Edwards's family seat in Hertfordshire.

All this—Queen Victoria, the bazaar, the Maidan, the Maharajah's palace, the rifle range, the reservoir, the Church, and the Zenana Mission; the humble bungalows where humble hopes were nourished and the stately houses where pride flourished; the Hostels, the Institute, the yards, the offices, and the Railway—all this was Jamalpur. J.M.P.

# THE
# FIRST
# SUNDAY

The first Sunday dawned with the suddenness of a sun impatient to kick aside the curtains of the night. The fervid beating of the tom-toms died out to give way to the heart-stopping cock-a-doodles of Mrs. Briggs's strutting back-garden cocks.

In the superintendent's European Grade Apprentices' Hostel bungalow, Mr. Knowles abruptly cut off a loud snore, not knowing what it was that had awakened him, although the same chanticleering woke him at precisely the same hour every day. He gazed about him bemusedly, then shook his sleeping wife's form urgently, having no regard for the peaceful look deep sleep had smoothed on her face.

"Come on, come on, Mother, time to get up."

Mrs. Knowles sat bolt upright, her mouth open in a yawn, her eyes closed. Her breath expelled deeply, and she slid sideways into a tightly curled ball. One arm moved of its own volition, grasping the sheet from curved fist to bent elbow, and her head was covered. Another deep sigh, and she continued to sleep.

"Mother, come along now, time to get a move on. Bakery to get going, new apprentices arriving for interviews and tests, and Solomon's no help—" As he spoke, Mr. Knowles was doing his deep-breathing exercises on the other side of the mosquito net. One-two—breathe in—three-four—

breathe out—"Mother—Mother—" he interspersed from time to time without thought.

Exercises over, he clapped his hands for hot water and cha, then pushed the mosquito net away from his wife's side of the bed. He shook her shoulder. "Mother—you've had five minutes."

Mrs. Knowles, defeated, sat up, yawning and scratching her hair. "What's the time then?"

"Late—late. Where's Solomon?" Mr. Knowles grumbled, pulling his dressing gown on.

"Worrying about his new wife, I dare say," Mrs. Knowles said, sliding her feet into cloth slippers. "Don't know what's got into him—should be used to it—she's his eighth at least."

In the servants' quarters Solomon unwrapped himself from his shrouding sheet, sat on the edge of his charpoy, scratching luxuriously, hawking and spitting vigorously onto the floor. Ayee, a man with a new wife slept like a baby, soft and deep, his loins worn out with exaltation, his seed planted in her youthful garden.

His foot prodded the slight form curled up in sleep on the floor beside his lordly couch. "Up, you light of my eyes, you delight of my groin, see if you can serve me damn quick time, with water for my person and hot cha for my dryness."

Two large, fawnlike eyes gazed at him, then were veiled before he could read their expression. The slight form rolled away from the prodding foot, taking its covering sheet to preserve a modesty that had not been there during the intimate night.

Solomon stared at the huddled figure, scowling. A man may speak tenderly in the night, but when the cock crowed, he had to speak with authority, with coldness lest his woman forget he was her lord.

"Where are the rippling waves of hair I dreamed of burying my face in, flower-garlanded and sweet-scented? Do not the women gossip of Solomon's wife, the comfort of his old-age, the beauty to lighten his days, combing and dressing her hair hourly until it shines like a panther's coat, whilst they keel the pots? Ayee, where are the dulcet tones lifted in song to ease my tired mind from its labours? All I see is a screwed-up loaf of hair—and what do I hear? A whimpering hoarse sound fit only for a mewing cat."

Her head remained bowed; she did not move. He spat again. Taking his lotah, he removed himself to the back lane to crouch over the open ditch, one of a long line of figures intent on relieving themselves.

"Salaam, Lord," cringed Francis Baker.

Solomon ignored him. "These low-born sons of buffalo, do they not know it is not seemly to look on their betters when they are privately occupied?" he muttered to himself, gazing remotely into space with as much cool authority as he could muster while squatting on the ground over a fetid ditch. Business done, he scooped his hand in the water in the lotah and cleansed himself. One hand for cleansing, one hand for eating. It was the way.

Presently, refreshed by tea and dressed in splendour, as became the head bearer of a large establishment, he addressed his silent wife. "I go now. Whilst I am away, busy yourself with woman's work. See that my uniform of yesterday is given to dhobi for quick return. Sit with the women. The wife of the head gardener is wise—watch her, learn from her. Walk with downcast eyes. There is much evil in towns. Avoid it. You are wife of head bearer now. You cannot bring shame on one so elevated. Keep your village ways for a village. Such monies I, Solomon, have paid for you."

Strutting back and forth, his coloured sash-ends swinging, Solomon's voice was filling with importance. Chandhi, surprised, unwisely retorted, "Monies you have paid for me? Did not my father pay you dowry?"

"Aye, woman—do not interrupt—"

"Such grandness he paid for," Chandhi uttered. "One slave quarter, one common stove for all. No field for shitting in, only drain for all castes and kinds—such greatness, your honour."

Solomon gasped. "Such language! Such shame! I have been deceived."

Emboldened by his weakness, Chandhi continued. "Where are the riches I was promised? Nothing but food from the white man's leavings—like dogs we are fed. Where is my garden? Only pilfered offerings I get from the white woman's garden. Thieves and dogs, that is what we are." Her eyes flashed and met his fearlessly.

Solomon swelled up. "Big we are getting, and proud! But am I not Solomon? Have I not a rope to chide thee with?"

He withdrew with dignity, drawing himself up outside his quarters so all who glanced his way could see how splendid he looked in his fine bearer's uniform. "Francis, ho, Francis," he called, imitating Mr. Knowles's air of authority.

A shadow detached itself from the banyan tree. Francis Baker, a thin, crooked shape, slid up to Solomon, moving like a cringing animal in a fawning, belly-to-the-ground manner. "Here, Solomon, I am here." He bobbed his black-capped head and smiled ingratiatingly.

Solomon needed to feel important. His wife should have let him leave his house as a lord. She should have shown him proper abasement, proper respect, as was his due. Was she not an ignorant village girl? And was he not Solomon, head bearer for Mr. Knowles? Was he not a man of the town, a Railway man? Without immediately speaking to Francis, he walked as if in deep thought towards the banyan tree.

He paused. "Francis, you of the thugs, you owe me much for silence. Do I not know many things?"

Francis' face twisted. He glanced about him uneasily., "Urimi, Solomon. Are there not ears in the very stones? What art thou trying to do?"

"Rest easy. I do not betray." Solomon nodded importantly. "But I know, and thou knowest, whom the police want for the merchant found dead on the Grand Trunk Road. Very dead, he was, and his pockets very empty. Then there is the matter of the bazaar whore. You drink, Francis, and when you drink you talk." Solomon smiled into his companion's murderous eyes. "I have in my village a letter. Ayee—anything happens to me—" he paused meaningfully. "You are top-class baker, Francis. You are also a jackal and see much."

Francis stared at Solomon. "Ayee, that is true. I see much." He tried to make something sinister of his reply, not knowing in which direction Solomon was taking this uncomfortable conversation.

"Worried I am about Chandhi, my new wife. I am Solomon, Head Bearer. I cannot lose face. Watch her, Francis, and report. Watch honestly. Lies about her I do not want."

"You have a feeling?"

"I have a feeling. I see looks from the other women. Sly smiles. And the other bearers are unusually insolent."

Francis nodded. "I will watch. Nothing I have heard. But then, none seek me out to gossip." He smiled, as if this were a compliment to the fear he sought to instil in others.

Solomon inclined his head grandly. "I go now to Knowles sahib. This is between us."

Francis watched him go and smiled. "You inflated bladder of emptiness. One twist, and you are an empty bladder," he muttered, scratching his crotch. Ayee, would Chandhi pay him for silence? If she were Charlie's new wife, Laksmi, the thought would be very sweet. Laksmi was young and tender, her belly and breasts round as melons, her mouth as red as a pomegranate. But Chandhi—Francis spat. The sharpness of her tongue could cut a man's member in two. Uri, uri, such thinking was painful.

Time to work. "Pheelip, Pheelip, you dressed-up pimp, where art thou? Works begins." Francis limped into the bakery.

Philip, his assistant, was tending the huge stoves, singing in a rich tenor, "By the moon's silveree light . . . Hi'll be larving you tonight. . . ."

"Ho, Pheelip, we are not nigger men any more," Francis mocked. "We are sahibs and must mouth their womenfolks' nonsense. Larving you, indeed. And who is it you are larving, Pheelip? Who are you honouring with your white man's clothes, your foul scentings, and now your singing? A white woman, eh?"

"Francis, you're late," Mrs. Knowles declared, emerging from a large walk-in pantry. "There's lots to do."

Francis banged the bread tins viciously on the newly scrubbed tables and then silence reigned as Mrs. Knowles weighed out the flour and discussed the number of loaves needed for the Hostel and the local Railway houses.

"So many cakes," grumbled Francis. "Is there to be a big tamasha that so many fine cakes are needed? Where is the time?"

Philip's eyes shone. "Many fine sahibs coming, many old women feed their bellies. Make bellies heavy, can't move. Have time to notice fine female form." He rolled his eyes and outlined a female figure behind Mrs. Knowles's back with his hands and wriggled his hips.

"You are perhaps noticing Chandhi, the new wife of Solomon?" queried Francis slyly as Mrs. Knowles washed her hands and left. He watched Philip's face for a sign.

"Chandhi, that moon-faced cow! Nay, brother, where are your eyes? There are more delights on hand than that." Philip laughed. So assured he sounded that Francis narrowed his eyes. Was he missing something?

Next to the bakery was the large kitchen, designed to feed one thousand apprentices. Charlie Cook, a yellow-faced, squat figure, was discussing the day's menu with Solomon and Mr. Knowles.

"Meat will have to be minced, or curry," Charlie insisted. "New butcher no good. Bif he send not from cow, probably police line mules. He is son of Shaitan." He banged the offending meat with his knife. "Black it is like his evil soul. No ros-bif today, too tough. He get bif contract, then supply the leather of his shoes."

Mr. Knowles surveyed the offending meat. "Looks all right to me. Roast beef always on Sunday. Come on, Charlie," he cajoled. "What's wrong with you?"

"No can do," grumbled Charlie. "Ros-bif for pukka sahib-log. These log chilli-crack, not pukka. What they know of ros-bif, Yorkshire pudden? Curry better. No cutting, no swallow. Little bif in curry, rest cutlet in gravy, very good. Tomorrow, sahib, you see badmash butcher, tell him no more goat, bufflow or mule—only cow. I am first-class cook, not magician."

Mr. Knowles shrugged. "Tough or not tough, roast beef it has to be. You are a good cook, Charlie, you'll manage. You know Mr. Grundy Principal and Mr. Nightingale are coming to see the new apprentice sahibs. What are they going to say if they see curry on Sunday and no roast beef? Cutlets from left-overs," he added as he left quickly, giving the stubborn gleam in Charlie's eye no time to convert into further argument.

Solomon accompanied Mr. Knowles, who continued grumbling, "Marriage certainly doesn't seem to bring joy. Here you are, Solomon, with a face as long as a fiddle, and Charlie, married for the first time, as miserable as sin."

"Women not the same any more, sahib—not docile. We have vipers in our bosoms, making eyes all over the place and not recognising duty."

"Chandhi giving you trouble, eh, Solomon?"

"Ayee. The things she say to me, sahib—such insolence from a wife! The trouble is, she too beautiful," Solomon declared mournfully. "Little wonder other bad men eyeing her with lustfulness."

Mr. Knowles looked at him sideways, but apart from a harrumph, said nothing. Chandhi was not his idea of a beauty. Face too round, like a cow.

At Number 42 Prince's Road, next door to the Armoury and Regimental offices, Sergeant-Major Barhill, Mrs. Barhill, and their daughter, Jane, were at breakfast. Sergeant-Major Barhill was a large, unyielding chunk of a man, with a fiery face and small eyes like unreflecting brown pebbles. His sweeping moustache was magnificent, contrasting with his closely cropped salt-and-pepper hair. At home he was a bully. His wife had been lovely once, in a washed-out English way, but her years in India and her husband's constant criticism had worn her down. Having a way with ladies (the silly bitches, if only they knew, his wife thought bitterly) and with many affairs under his belt (dirty old beast, thought his daughter scornfully), he was terrified of his daughter's astonishing beauty, full of dark thoughts of incest, wildly jealous at the idea of another man possessing her. His confusion had led him to suppose that Jane was a harlot and that all the men in the Station had rape on their minds where she was concerned.

She was slim and vital, her glowing auburn hair and slanting hazel eyes shining with health; she had a determined tilt to her chin and a long-legged stride. Somehow, her proportions, the structure of her bones, the relationship of eyes to nose, to mouth, to cheeks had grown more perfect as she had blossomed from an almost ugly child to a beautiful woman—one who was not yet aware of her power. Like a sleeping tigress waiting to strike, her mother sometimes thought, wondering what went on behind her daughter's calm facade.

Jane had had a good education and was an excellent musician, having spent most of her life as a boarder in a convent high in the Himalayas, where the air was clean and pure and where she was safe from the prying eyes and desires of men. The nuns had recommended that she go to England to study at the Royal College of Music, to which she had won a scholarship. "Out of the question!" her father had bellowed, instantly withdrawing her from school.

Now she had no life of her own to speak of. Her letters were opened and, more often than not, destroyed. She was not permitted to invite friends to her home unless her father first approved them; and since he had the tendency to force himself upon those he approved (he only approved pretty young gals), Jane never proffered invitations, which tended to give her the reputation of being stand-offish. Since coming home from school it was insisted that she go nowhere unless accompanied by one, or, preferably, both her parents. Even at night she was never alone, since her ayah, her shadow, was on hand to guard her and report all her movements. A job, of course, was out of the question, but the Maharajah (who admired Mrs. Barhill for her dedicated work at a small hospital he had founded) had persuaded Jane's parents to allow her to teach his young daughters the piano. Her twice-weekly trips to the palace (under escort) and playing the organ at church were her chief activities.

"Going to church, I suppose," Sergeant-Major Barhill sneered. "Well, see your daughter gets behind the organ and stays there. I want her playing hymns, not playing around, d'ye hear?"

"Yes," his wife replied shortly.

"And don't tell me that nothing can happen at church, because I know different."

Mrs. Barhill sliced through her boiled egg as if she wished it were her husband's neck. She said nothing.

The Sergeant-Major wasn't done yet. "No hanging around after, gossiping with those old biddies you call your friends. More goes on when you are tearing others to pieces than you could imagine with your limited intelligence. When the cats are off, the mice are having it—and I mean, *having* it." He glared around the table. "I've noticed that slimy Sergeant O'Leary leering around." His teeth bared briefly at the malicious pun. "He needn't think he's making a cuckoo out of me, dropping his bastards on my doorstep."

Foolishly, Mrs. Barhill gawped at him. "Sergeant O'Leary? If he comes here, surely it's only to see you. You do work together. I can't imagine what you're getting at— everyone knows of his disgusting affair with Mrs. Ray. Surely you're not suggesting—"

"Suggesting? No, I'm not suggesting—I'm telling you, you stupid bag. There are plenty more fish in the sea besides Mrs. Ray, and he's not angling in my pond, so watch it, if you have eyes anywhere besides your backside."

"I can't imagine why—" Mrs. Barhill foolishly began again, her face working painfully.

"Of course you can't imagine—you never had any imagination," the Sergeant-Major roared, slamming the table with a solid fist. Jane stood up. "Sit down!" he bellowed. "You stay there and get it into your head—I'm not having any tykes creeping round here like dogs after a bitch in heat. I know men. Only one thing on their minds, and it's generally found south of the navel."

Jane sat frozen. I hate him, hate him, hammered through her brain. He's a filthy goat, thinks every man is just like himself, one face for home, another for the world. As if I'd let that slimy little rat Sergeant O'Leary near me. As she thought of Sergeant O'Leary and his groping hands, his eyes that fastened on either her breasts or groin, she reddened.

Her father glared at her. "Got muck on your face, haven't you?"

"Muck?" She stared at him bemusedly.

"Yes, muck, paint, tart's icing. You've been and painted your face. I'm not having any daughter of mine going around like a painted whore. Slut! Jezebel!"

"But I haven't—"

"Don't answer me back, you painted whore. Ayah!" he roared. "Ayah!"

"Sahib, sahib," Ayah called as she came running.

"Take missie and see she washes her face."

"Ehdum, sahib."

As Jane left the room, her back rigid with fury, her father yelled after her, "Scrub it, damn you, and no more muck, or I'll take sandpaper to it myself."

Ayah followed Jane to the bathroom. She splashed water about, her bangles jangling. "What for sahib say you paint face? My missie baba got good colour, no need paint." She splashed more water. "Eh, eh, don't cry."

"I'm not crying," Jane sobbed furiously. "I hate him, I hate him."

"You big missie now. Ayah know. But Ayah getting blind, no can see everything, no can see what missie do all the time." She winked. "You listen Ayah, Ayah help." She dried her hands. "Face clean, eh?" She winked again. "Come dress, church time."

Jane hugged her, feeling the silk of her sari slip beneath her cheek. She could smell musk and garlic and soap. "You're a treasure. You'll always be there, won't you?"

"Shee shee, baba. Ayah will always be here."

"I don't think I can put up with him much longer—God, how Mother stands it—he's knocked all the spirit out of her."

Ayah clicked her tongue. "Men all same, big noise, like wind." She patted Jane's hand. "Come, pretty frock, missie, look pretty for church."

Before leaving for the church service, Mrs. Barhill, Jane, and Ayah lined up for inspection.

"Your seams are crooked," Sergeant-Major Barhill barked at his wife. "But I expect that's better than odd stockings, which is not unusual for you." He glared at Jane. "Where d'ja get that hat? Too saucy by half. Change it."

"Can't," Jane said flatly. "It's the only one I have. It's my school felt."

"Well, you've tarted it up," he said, refusing to admit he was wrong. "What's all that ribbon and stuff?"

"The hat band. With the school colours."

"Wear your beret. Won't have every Tom, Dick, and Harry eyeing your damned hat like moths to a candle."

Jane deliberately set her beret at a provocative angle over one eye, stared moodily at her reflection in the mirror, and reappeared.

Her father frowned. "That's worse. What's wrong with you, girl? Going out of your way to annoy me?"

Jane reappeared in the hat, and after a few minor adjustments, which included pinning her collar together, lest the pulse beating in the nape of her throat should give the dogs after her scent any ideas, the three women were ready to leave. On foot, they joined the stream of worshippers, some answering the loud bells of the C. of E. church, others separating at Edward Road to make their way towards the subdued tinkle of the Roman Catholic chimes.

Mrs. Barhill was soon lost in conversation with her cronies—Mrs. Maughan, Mrs. Darsi Jones, Mrs. Fitter Jones, all of them envied covenanted ladies. They walked on, chatting vigorously, while Jane and Ayah trailed behind. A soldier trotted by, easy in the saddle. His back was straight, his legs muscular in jodhpurs. How splendid he was. Jane's heart pounded unsteadily. What would it be like with a man—a proper man? Rebelliously, she yearned for freedom. As long as her father was alive she would not be permitted to meet men, go out with one, marry. Her future was bleak. She would die an old maid. Angry tears filled her eyes, and, annoyed, she brushed them away with her wrist.

On arriving at the church the ladies filed into their seats. Mrs. Barhill had forgotten Jane, who made her way to the organ, followed by Ayah, who crouched at her feet, muttering to herself. Mrs. Pritchard, the Vicar's wife, approached.

"I have the music ready, all dear Cuthbert's favourites. He won't be sorry to go. He is basically a missionary, dear boy, and this place, this way of life—so easy, so comfortable—is not his cup of tea."

Jane had no idea what she was talking about, but reached out her hand for the sheets of music, smiling automatically.

"I know you know it all, my dear, such a wonderful organist. If it weren't for *God*, I'd say you were wasted here." Mrs. Pritchard smiled vaguely and moved away to greet the three Zenana Virgins. Dressed in long grey frocks and grey silk veils, they were moving with assurance up the aisle to their pews at the front.

Miss Harris was in the lead, pink-cheeked, crippled, beaming like a good-natured cherub, leaning heavily on her stick. She waved her hand with a languid gesture at selected acquaintances, rather like royalty. Behind her came gaunt, fanatical Miss Blenkinsop, who had her gaze firmly fixed on the cross on the altar as the knights of old would have gazed at the Holy Grail, had they ever found it. She clutched her Bible to her meagre breasts and murmured a sequence more suited to the R.C. church down the road. Behind her crept young Miss Toogood, nervous and bewildered, apt to trip over her large feet. A vacant grin was pinned on her colourless face as she bobbed and curtsied left and right, regardless of whether the recipients of her courtesy were desirables, acknowledged by Miss Harris and Miss Blenkinsop, or undesirables who had no place in the church at all. Closely behind the three Virgins came Mrs. Ray, hip-thrusting, prancing.

Mrs. Pritchard's welcoming smile faded; her eyes widened with pain, then closed. What would dear Cuthbert think, what was the world coming to, when females like Mrs. Ray took to churchgoing? Grateful that the intruder was behind the Zenana ladies, Mrs. Pritchard took Miss Harris by the arm and led her to their reserved pew. Miss Blenkinsop and Miss Toogood followed. The four of them knelt to pray.

A scrap of black velvet graced Mrs. Ray's dyed red mane. She clutched Sergeant O'Leary's arm in a vice-like grip; her enamelled and brightly painted face was turned towards his, her heavily mascaraed eyes gazing up into his soulfully. Her heels were very high, her skirt short, showing off a pair of exquisitely shaped calves.

"My goodness me," gasped Mrs. Fitter Jones, "Just look at that dress. I do declare the hussy hasn't a stitch on underneath, and chiffon, too."

"No respect, that's what," said Mrs. Darsi Jones. "I can't look at her. Not decent, is it, and this a church. Wouldn't be allowed in chapel, it wouldn't."

"Crack her face if she smiles," sniffed Mrs. Maughan. "Can't complain of her lack of drawers, you can't," she added. "Wonderful she actually remembered to put on anything at all. My bearer was telling me she wears nothing at all at home."

"In front of her bearer? Surely not!" exclaimed Mrs. Barhill, aghast, but secretly wondering what else went on in that direction.

"She thinks nothing of it," announced Mrs. Maughan. "Says servants should walk around with their eyes shut and their minds on their work."

"That may be so," said Mrs. Darsi Jones. "But receiving visitors—all and sundry—in the altogether, now, that's another matter."

"Receives visitors?" gasped Mrs. Barhill. "In the altogether? No!"

"Yes! Stark naked, but not quite like a newborn baby," grimly proclaimed Mrs. Darsi Jones. "Wonderful sight, don't you think?"

"French, her background is," said Mrs. Fitter Jones, as if that explained everything.

The four ladies squeezed down to make room at the end of their pew for Mrs. Knowles and her daughter, Mary.

"Good God, girl!" Mrs. Barhill said, stunned. "Where did you get that hat? Like a Chinese pagoda, it is. All it misses are bells."

"Nice, isn't it?" said Mary. "Quite the latest thing—got it in the Army and Navy." She fluffed up her hair.

"Army and Navy! Never!" said Mrs. Barhill disbelievingly. "The Sergeant-Major would have a fit if he thought they sold hats like that. Never let me shop there again."

Mary giggled. "He'll love it, good sport he is."

"Quite a sensation it's caused," said Mrs. Fitter Jones. "Did you see Mrs. Ray eyeing it as you passed?"

"She could have killed O'Leary when he whistled at me outside," Mary giggled. "But that was no compliment—who wants him anyway?"

Mrs. Knowles laughed. "You are naughty, Mary—but at least you have sense."

The ladies stood up respectfully as Mr. Edwards, self-appointed elder of the church, with candlestick held high, led Mr. Papworth, Mr. Nightingale, and Mr. Grundy to their pews. Their wives, of no importance whilst their lords and masters were around, followed abjectly, to take their places, as was right, in lower pews. Not even for wives was it permitted the honor of sharing a pew with the rulers of the Railway.

In church not all men are created equal in the eyes of the Lord, Jane thought as her pedalling feet swelled the organ into majestic sound. At least, not in this church.

As soon as the great men had seated themselves, looking neither to right nor left, nor bowing their heads to the cross, the vicar appeared. The Reverend Pritchard was a small, wizened, yellow man, face and head wealed with scars, and, it was revealed modestly by his wife, not a single hair grew anywhere on his body.

"Real saint, he is," breathed Mrs. Darsi Jones. "Lucky he is to be alive. Just imagine to have actually been inside a cannibal pot."

"Don't fancy eating him, myself," grunted Mrs. Maughan. "Too dried up by half, worse than the bazaar fowls."

Mrs. Knowles shook with silent laughter. "Wonder what he looks like in the altogether—did Mrs. Pritchard say exactly?"

"Oh, wicked you are," whispered Mrs. Darsi Jones.

"It's romantic you are," retorted Mrs. Fitter Jones. "Cannibal pots, indeed—don't know where you get your yarns from."

"True it is, New Guinea it was, real savages they are," Mrs. Darsi Jones protested. She coloured and shut up hurriedly as the Honourable Bertram Papworth, turning his head very slowly, glared at her.

Oh, my goodness, done it I have, Dylan will kill me, she thought while Mary Knowles winked at him and shook her hat enchantingly. Bertram Papworth looked startled, then gratified. A gleam appeared in his eye and a kind of promising half-leer, before, with a hurried harrumph, he turned round to face front, only the ruddy colouration of his neck above starched collar revealing the anticipatory nature of his passion.

"Ooh, look at your Jane." Mrs. Darsi Jones nudged Mrs. Barhill. "How did he get there? It's furious, I reckon Mrs. Ray is."

"Madame is not pleased," Mrs. Maughan announced, grinning like a well-fed cat as she craned her neck around. "Her enamel has cracked, what a picture. Wouldn't like to be in Jane's shoes after the service."

Jane sat at the organ in agony, similar thoughts flashing through her mind while she forced herself to concentrate on "Jerusalem." Sergeant O'Leary had edged his way up to the organ, subtly avoiding detection by sneaking from pillar to pillar, and was fussing over the pages of a music book.

Helplessly, Mrs. Barhill gazed at her besieged daughter. It was too much, too much. Suppose the Sergeant-Major took it into his head to sneak into church, checking up on his womenfolk? It was like him, he'd done it before, and oh God, he'd kill them, beat them senseless with that big leather strap of his.

"Oh dear, oh dear, the Sergeant-Major will turn up, I know he will," Mrs. Barhill whispered in panic to Mrs. Maughan. "He'll be furious. But what can I do, I can't make a scene."

"I don't think you'll have to," said Mrs. Knowles cheerfully, settling back to enjoy the drama, unaware of the true nature of life in the Barhill establishment. "Mrs. Ray will do it for you, wait and see."

All eyes in the church were on Sergeant O'Leary and Jane. A few people turned from time to time to observe Mrs. Ray's fury, while the Reverend Pritchard fought hard to draw his flock's attention back to God.

"Go away," Jane hissed, shaking O'Leary's arm from around her shoulders. He smelled horribly of Brylcreem and foxes. Sex smells like that, she suddenly realised in a wave of intuition. Mrs. Ray and he had *done it*, then had come straight to church, sweaty, without even washing, oh God, how disgusting.

"Go away," she hissed again, trying to wriggle to the edge of the stool. "Leave me alone."

"I can't," whispered O'Leary, trying to look soulful, like Valentino. His eyes rolled horribly. "From the first moment I looked into your green eyes, I was lost, a drowned man."

"Rubbish," Jane cried, striking a jarring chord. She pedalled furiously.

"It's true, it's true, oh my love, I can't eat or sleep—all night I see your lovely face—all night I dream of holding you close—"

"Rubbish," Jane repeated. "You say that to every woman you meet—don't think I don't know about toads like you."

"Would you refuse a starving man?" O'Leary demanded. "Not another morsel will cross my lips until you let me possess you."

"Horrible, horrible man," Jane cried. "Just go away. Leave me alone. I don't like you."

"Don't be shy," O'Leary pressed. "Today, girls don't have to pretend. I was never one for modesty, anyway."

"Ohh!" Jane hissed. Another jarring chord. She looked towards Ayah. Why didn't the foolish woman do something?

Ayah sat on her haunches, her face buried in the folds of her sari. Uri, uri, what was a native woman to do? She could not strike an Englishman, a white man. She could not even order him to go. She rocked back and forth and moaned.

"Oh heavens," whispered Mrs. Maughan delightedly. "Just watch Mrs. Ray."

Fascinated, all eyes turned on Mrs. Ray. She made her way from pew to pew with an odd sliding motion, almost walking on her haunches, maintaining a height equal to the seated members of the congregation. She reached the Honourable Bertram Papworth's pew at the same moment as the Reverend Pritchard mounted the steps of the pulpit to begin his sermon. Sliding sideways with a quick, furtive flip of her hips, she sat down, all the while gazing ahead as if nothing were unusual about her curious behaviour.

Mr. Papworth, that worthy, turned to gaze at her as if she were some undesirable from the bazaar. He rose, pushed past the intruder, and stalked down the aisle towards the back of the church. Mr. Nightingale, Mr. Grundy, and the three wives stared after him, then at each other, then rose and hurried after him. All eyes turned from the drama unfolding at the front of the church to watch the Railway steam out of sight.

Up in his pulpit, the Reverend Pritchard watched with an air of complete bewilderment. Helplessly, he turned the pages of the Bible, then directed his childlike eyes towards his wife. But she was watching Mrs. Ray with an expression of pure venom.

By now Mrs. Ray had arrived at the organ, although the crossing before the altar had not been without peril.

"You have to admire her," declared Mrs. Knowles. "Why, she practically crawled on her hands and knees. What does she think she is, a mole?"

"I'd like to see the Zenana Virgins' faces," said Mrs. Maughan with relish. "They must have had a ringside view of her naked bum."

"Mrs. Maughan, it's rude you are," said Mrs. Fitter Jones, laughing.

"Hush!" said Mrs. Barhill frantically. Lord, oh Lord, she should have stayed in bed this morning. Jane should have stayed in bed this morning. Her ears strained to listen to what was being said at the organ.

"George!" hissed Mrs. Ray. "If you don't leave her alone, I'll kill you."

Jane sat with downcast eyes, hands folded in her lap. Would the sermon never start? The church was quiet as a tomb.

O'Leary made no reply, merely turning his back on Mrs. Ray to gaze at the sky through the rose window. She grasped his arm. "Hey, you listen to me, I'm your woman, damn you. You'd better not forget it."

"Go away," O'Leary said distinctly.

"Go away! Who the hell d'you think you're talking to?" Mrs. Ray's voice rose shrilly. "You bastard! What's been going on here?"

"Tell her, dear," suggested O'Leary, leaning over Jane.

"Oh!" Jane gasped. Before she realised what was happening, her quiescent hand flew from her lap to strike a violent blow against Brylcreem, fox-musk, and her subjection to this indignity.

"Chela jao, bad man," suddenly shrilled Ayah. Her flailing arms pushed Mrs. Ray and Sergeant O'Leary from the organ. "Go, go, missie baba not want buffalo droppings like you under her nose, she fine, good girl."

Finding the situation quite beyond him, the Reverend Pritchard hurriedly gave the last blessing from the pulpit before the service had really begun and retired to the sanctuary, where he absentmindedly emptied the chalice of all the communion wine.

"Well, I never," said Miss Harris audibly when it became apparent that the service was over, then blushed as Miss Blenkinsop glared frigidly at her.

"Come," said Miss Blenkinsop, sweeping down the aisle. As the three ladies left the church, Miss Blenkinsop was heard to remark that if she hurried, she could catch the rest of the service at the R.C. church, where Father Millet ran a far tighter ship.

"Wants her tipple," Mrs. Knowles remarked.

"Wonder if that's where the Honourable Bertram went," said Mrs. Maughan.

"Jane will want me," Mrs. Barhill said, thanking God that her worst fears had not been realised. Then she stopped dead in her tracks and moaned piteously. She wasn't safe yet. Her husband was sure to hear of this morning's circus, and no doubt the details would be greatly exaggerated by then. Whatever happened, Jane would not be thought the guiltless party she was.

Oh dear, oh dear. Mrs. Barhill hurried towards her precious child, hopefully wondering if they could swear the entire congregation to secrecy.

Outside the church, groups gathered together, heads nodding vigorously as they discussed the latest scandal, a scandal that in fact was still in the making as Mrs. Ray and her renegade lover argued passionately on the wide sweep where all the carriages waited and horses twitched nervously.

"Poor man, what a last service," Mrs. Knowles said, looking about for the Reverend Pritchard.

"At least he will never forget us," said Mrs. Maughan.

"Indeed, it was unusual," decided Mrs. Darsi Jones. "Quite excited, I got."

"Poor Jane," continued Mrs. Knowles. "She's such a quiet little thing." She laughed. "Who would want O'Leary to fall in love with them, anyway?"

"It's no compliment, at any rate," said Mrs. Fitter Jones. "Me, I'd rather remain a spinster."

The Reverend Pritchard and his wife approached. "Ladies, ladies, I'm so sorry," cried the vicar.

"Sorry? Why?" asked Mrs. Knowles.

"I forgot to take Holy Communion, entirely forgot," the Reverend moaned. "My last service amongst you all—and I forgot it." He hiccoughed gently.

Mrs. Knowles started to say that they, at least, would never forget this last service, then thought better of it. Instead she said, "We'll miss you, Reverend Pritchard. It won't be the same without you."

"I'll be here in spirit," he said. Somehow the word "spirit" caused him to blush, and he started humming gently to himself.

"Why, here comes Jane," said Mrs. Pritchard brightly.

Jane smiled wanly at them. "I'm sorry," she said uncertainly.

"Nymphs and shepherds, come away, come away," hummed the Reverend Pritchard.

"Why, Jane, my dear girl, it wasn't your fault," said Mrs. Pritchard. "It was *theirs*—" She nodded towards the carriages, refusing to look at the arguing couple.

"Come, come, come away..." sang the Reverend Pritchard.

"That horrible little man deserves to be shot," said Mrs. Knowles stoutly.

"They both should be shot," said Mrs. Maughan. "The lower classes have no right to foist themselves upon us— look what happens when they do."

As if on cue, Mrs. Ray started to scream wildly, then got down on her knees and clutched O'Leary's trousered legs.

"Oh my God," said Mrs. Knowles.

"Let's turn our back on them—we can pray for them later," said Mrs. Pritchard. "Though you would think that they would take their business elsewhere. I'm sure God doesn't want it."

"Come, come, come away..." sang the Reverend Pritchard, sitting down on a carriage step. The carriage contained Miss Harris and Miss Toogood. They were talking earnestly in low voices and seemed surprised when the vicar deposited himself at their feet without invitation. Of Miss Blenkinsop, there was no sign.

Somehow, her husband's little song seemed to have unconsciously penetrated Mrs. Pritchard's mind, for impulsively, she suddenly drew Jane to her with both hands. "Come with us, child," she cried. "Come to New Zealand— there is nothing for you here, so much narrowness, so much putting Mammon before God. Your soul will be crippled here—let it soar—come with us."

"I can't," said Jane. "My father wouldn't allow it." Her flat answer concealed the astonishment she suddenly felt. Go to New Zealand? The idea was incredible.

"If you truly desired it, your father would not stand in your way."

You don't know my father, Jane thought, but knew Mrs. Pritchard would not understand such a remark. "It's a big decision to make so suddenly," she said instead.

"Sometimes, when your soul is thirsty, you must act with your heart and not your mind," Mrs. Pritchard cried eagerly.

"Mrs. Pritchard, I really appreciate it—I'm deeply touched," Jane stumbled. "But I don't think I'm ready for New Zealand."

Mary Knowles joined them. "Walk back with you, Jane?"

The two girls shook hands with Mrs. Pritchard and glanced doubtfully towards the Reverend Pritchard. "Say goodbye to him," said Jane.

"Not goodbye yet," said Mrs. Pritchard. "We don't leave until tomorrow. Let us know if you change your mind."

"I will," Jane promised.

"Come on, Jane," urged Mary, who had been staring over Jane's shoulder. "O'Leary's shaken off Madame and will make a beeline for you."

"Oh God," Jane groaned. "Let's run. Quick!"

"Missie baba—missie baba—" Ayah cried, suddenly waking up to the fact that her young mistress was rushing pell-mell down the road.

Observing that Sergeant O'Leary was about to set off in pursuit, Mrs. Darsi Jones and Mrs. Fitter Jones moved smoothly into action, cornering him and asking, in the nagging tones of old wives, what did he think he was playing at, causing such a scene in church, and if he didn't want his commanding officer to find out, he'd better think twice about it in the future. By the time the lecture had run its course, Jane and Mary had vanished.

Miss Harris and Miss Toogood had concluded their discussion, and now Miss Harris looked about her. Spotting Mrs. Knowles, she climbed down from the carriage, taking care not to step upon the vicar, who had lapsed into *H.M.S. Pinafore* ("I am the ruler of the Queen's Navee, tiddly pom pom pom . . ."), and buttonholed her.

"Mrs. Knowles, a word in your ear," she said.

Mrs. Knowles paused, surprised. She could not recollect ever having spoken with any of the Virgins.

"I am Miss Harris. That is Miss Toogood. She is rather delicate and needs fresh air and exercise. Would you be good enough to take her under your wing and let her ride with you when you bicycle around the Maidan? We have frequently observed you, and conclude it is a regular habit with you."

"Why yes, it is—"

"We thought so," Miss Harris interrupted smoothly. "I am too old, besides being crippled with arthritis. Miss Blenkinsop does not bicycle. Too frivolous. It would be charitable of you."

Mrs. Knowles agreed, then asked, "Is not Miss Toogood somewhat nervous?"

"She is," said Miss Harris. "Exercise, we are certain, will improve her nerves. One cannot live in India unless one's nerves are strong." She bowed politely and climbed back into her carriage, assisted by the horseman.

"She looks like a Dutch doll, but I'd say that one is a tough old biddy," Mrs. Knowles declared.

"Do themselves well," said Mrs. Briggs ingratiatingly. She lived behind the Apprentices' Hostel and supplied most households with good English eggs. "Mr. Briggs went up there, to the Mission, to look at their plumbing. Sunken baths, real W.C.s with their own cesspit. No thunder boxes for them, or tin tubs like the rest of us. You should have heard him when he came home—says if he comes back after this life, he'll come back as a missionary. Notice their horses? Got six, they have—and a beautiful car."

The ladies looked at each other. "Car? I've never seen a car, and I go to see them often," declared Mrs. Pritchard.

"Yes, car," said Mrs. Briggs, satisfied with the stir she was creating. "A real beauty: the old one got it on the last visit she made to the old country, giving lectures on their work and appealing for funds. Bet the folk that raised the wind to help the savages didn't know it was for a motor to shift them around in style. Got a chauffeur with a swank livery, too," she added for good measure.

"Then why don't they use it, if only to put Papworth's nose out of joint?" asked Mrs. Knowles.

"Waiting for the Bishop to bless it, of course," said Mrs. Briggs. "They never do anything without the Bishop."

The ladies walked slowly back to their homes together.

"Four cars in the Station, my goodness," said Mrs. Barhill. "Just think, four cars now. Soon everyone will want them."

Arrived at Jane's house, Mary smiled up at Sergeant-Major Barhill. "I declare you get handsomer every day; never seen such marvellous mustachios. You going to the Apprentices' ball, Sergeant-Major?"

"Of course we are," he said, fingering the sweep of his

moustache. "Saving a dance for you, I am, my dear."

Mary looked at him wickedly. "I bet you're a wonderful dancer—most big men are."

The Sergeant-Major swelled with pride; his mustachios twirled furiously.

"You should see my dress," Mary continued, her eyes sparkling. "A broth of a dress, it is, midnight blue, backless, down to the ground."

"Backless?" asked the Sergeant-Major.

"Backless." Mary shivered. "There's something thrilling about dancing with a man and feeling his bare hand on your bare back, don't you think?" She drew her shoulders up and sighed. "Thrilling."

"Backless," mused the Sergeant-Major.

"You got Jane a dress yet?"

"No," he replied, his eyes hot on Mary's curving lips. "Jane doesn't dance."

"Of course she does! She had lessons galore at school—you know she did. Mrs. Barhill says you were always complaining about the bills. Don't want to waste all that money, do you?"

Jane was speechless with shock. If only she dared speak to her father like this. She envied Mary her easy relationship with her parents. But then, Mr. and Mrs. Knowles were normal people.

"Perhaps I should have said Jane doesn't like to dance," the Sergeant-Major conceded.

"Nonsense! Every girl likes to dance!" Mary pouted. "If you don't let Jane go, I won't go. There! You'll not get a dance with me."

"Well—"

"I knew you'd agree. Wonderful! I didn't want to miss dancing with my favourite man." Pressing home the advantage, Mary added, "And you must promise to buy her a real dress—a down-to-the-ground dress in the latest fashion. Her old school evening dress just won't do. We can't have the Railway women outdoing the Army women, can we?"

"Buy her a dress? A dance dress?" the Sergeant-Major repeated, stunned.

"The latest fashion, mind," Mary admonished. "Promise?" Her blue eyes smiled winningly into his. "You're the Sergeant-Major—your daughter must be a credit to you, mustn't she?"

"I promise!" he cried recklessly. "Cross my heart and hope to die." He stuck his finger in his mouth like a schoolboy and held it up. "I promise," he repeated.

"Wonderful! I knew you'd agree!" Mary stood on tiptoes and gave him a smacking kiss, while his eyes popped and his neck turned a fiery red. "I'll go with Jane and help her choose—it's got to be something special, her first dance dress." She turned from the Sergeant-Major and winked at Jane. "Cheerio, Jane—see you at the Institute tomorrow for the practice dance, must hold our own. We can go shopping after. Give her plenty of money," she flashed over her shoulder to the Sergeant-Major. "You can't skimp on a decent dress."

Jane waited for the axe to fall, but her father was gazing after Mary with a sentimental smile on his silly old face. "Speak to your mother about some decent rags," he muttered. "But make sure you do take Mary along—your mother's not good at fashions. Can't have Railway gals outdoing Army gals."


$B$ack at the Hostel, the day's baking was over. The delivery wallahs had filled their boxes and left. Solomon was busy with his army of bearers, preparing for lunch. Charlie Cook was deep in his cooking and supervising the kitchen staff. Philip carefully greased his hair down, brushed his shoes, and contemplated the result in a mirror. Francis watched him.

"I go for a cup of tea and smoke," announced Philip, sauntering out.

Francis made no gesture to show he had heard, but as soon as Philip left, he followed him, muttering, "Cup of tea, eh? Heard it called many things, but cup of tea, that's new."

At a distance, Philip swaggered along, singing a love song. He saw the wives of the servants sitting with their children. He called out cheekily to them, but Chandhi, sitting apart and snoring lustily, he ignored. His pace quickened until he was within a stone's throw of Charlie Cook's quarters. He stopped, puffed his cigarette casually, looked carefully around, then flicked the cigarette in the air before slipping quietly inside. The door closed. None of the women had noticed.

Francis followed and leant against the door, his ear to a crack. The deep overhang concealed him in its shadows.

"Your man is busy, it is safe," he heard Philip say. "We will not be disturbed." There was a long, heaving sigh. Silence.

"All night, all day, my beloved, I have yearned for you," Philip crowed deep in his throat. "Your hair gleams like light on the water; it is soft as the velvet the memsahib wears, as dark and delightful as silk through my fingers. Your eyes are like the gazelle's, your teeth as pearls, your breasts as the pomegranate . . . ayee . . . my loins ache for need of you . . . Laksmi . . . your name is as music. . . ." Philip's voice was panting now; Laksmi was uttering small cries.

Very pretty, thought Francis. He has a way with him. Women are fools to be taken in by such a quick worker. He must have learnt well from the white priests; these Christians have a trick or two, such things have I seen. Real sahib, he is; if he lives long enough, he'll probably end up white.

Listening some more in case he ever needed such tricks, Francis turned his eyes into the blinding sun, towards Chandhi. Like a heavy goat, she is, like unrisen dough, lumpy and dull. Solomon has been sold a pup. He grinned evilly. Who in their right senses would seduce that. Ayee, a man must be starving to risk blood spilling over such a one.

He stretched and stepped away from the door. Uri, Pheelip, I envy you, more than a slice you are having from Charlie Cook's loaf. He wandered off, then catching sight of Solomon in the distance, called out, "Ho, Solomon, a word."

Now it was his turn to spin the moment out, to not utter anything until they were within the shade of the banyan tree. Solomon waited in agony, dreading the news.

Francis turned, grinning like a monkey. "Your Chandhi is safe. Not interested in her, is our Pheelip. Other fish he has to fry. Busy he is, scattering his seed—but not in thy wife."

Solomon's face lit up.

"Others have new, young wives," Francis said slyly. "With flashing eyes that rove and tantalizing breasts like unto pomegranates." He sniggered. "Better a free seat in a whorehouse—that Pheelip is playing with fire." He strolled off, laughing.

Solomon shrugged his shoulders. Other wives were not his concern. Only if Chandhi was pure and unsullied, knowing no other member but his own inside her, was he satisfied. He was aware that Francis did not admire Chandhi's beauty—but young men were fools. Let them seek out the shallowness of a pretty face. Old men gained more from firm flesh, and much of it. Uri, his loins tingled, longing for the night.

On the far side of the Maidan was "The Nest," a sprawling bungalow set in two acres of land. The house was occupied by Mrs. Jameson, a large, elderly woman, completely crippled. She spent her days in a wheelchair pushed by her daughter, Jessie, and her only remaining servant, her Ayah. Mr. Jameson was what was politely termed a domiciled European. He had left the Railway to work for a coolie contractor. In his more stable days he had bought the land and built the bungalow. He planted orange groves, mangoes, litchi and guava trees. He had constructed runs for turkey, geese, hens, and ducks. Then, having fathered two children, he promptly lost interest and disappeared with the young daughter of an engine driver, never to be seen or heard of again.

Mrs. Jameson had managed, with the contrivance of one scheme after another, to educate her son, James, and see him established as a clerk in the Railway offices. Jessie, a mere girl, had suffered. She had attended the Railway School, which, under the capable tuition of the two Anderton sisters, took the children up to Standard Two, no further. It was expected that boarding school would do the rest; all respectable children were sent to boarding school. Jessie did not go to boarding school. Instead, after the second standard, she remained at home to care for the birds. It was her job to breed them, make sure snakes and disease did not polish off too many, and sell them for the highest possible price. The goats and cows were also her responsibility. Breeding, milking, tending, selling. In moments of crisis when the servants could not be paid, she took over their jobs, ruining her health, until now she was a pale, listless woman, used to nothing but drudgery.

Mrs. Jameson handled the harvesting of the fruit crops and the selling of them until polio had crippled her. She took in paying guests, and a worry they had been, flitting off without paying when her back was turned, lifting various items from the house before they slid into the night. With her mother confined to a chair, Jessie had picked and bottled fruit, negotiated with merchants in the bazaar, shaken off their greasy, fawning hands, waited on the non-paying guests—and watched other girls grow up, enjoy life, live.

She saw them dating, courting, marrying. None of that had come her way. The dancing, ball dresses, picnics, kisses—all had passed her by. She was sick of hearing women compliment her mother: "Such a good daughter, so devoted."

What did they know of her aching heart, her rebellious nature, the longings that grew more painful with every bitter year that passed? Life was sweeping by, glorious, bold. She cringed in its shadows, dust under its flying hooves. God, what would she give for one night of passion, to know what it was like to be a woman, to be waited on, to be caressed, to be adored. To be ravished.

How sick she was of her mother's whining demands, of the confounded clacking hens and gobbling turkeys, of the non-stop routine of milking and mucking out, of bottling fruit and haggling. Of never quite making enough to give a moment's respite from tradesmen's demands.

James, her brother, he had had everything. Clumsy, stupid James, with his never-ending stories of big-game hunting, wasting a fortune on his guns and his safaris. He had never offered to take her, never spent as much as a rupee on her, never introduced her to any of his bachelor friends. Now she was too old, bloom faded, doomed to be a spinster, fastened to her mother for ever.

All dear James ever did was to send them a hunk of venison from time to time when he felt guilty. He never came, rarely wrote, although he lived but half a mile away. And she knew perfectly well that when her mother made her push her to his house, James dived out of the back door and slunk off to the Institute.

Ayah was becoming difficult too. She had taken to smoking bhang and spent most of her time in a drugged oblivion, oblivious to calls, ignoring pleas for help. She squatted on the veranda where the breeze fanned her, her hooded eyes closed, rocking back and forth on her heels, crooning to herself. Who knows where she went and what dreams she dreamed?

Jessie had no patience with her, or with anything else. On this Sunday she had completed all her chores and all Ayah's, too, and damned if she was going to do another thing. Ignoring her mother's ringing and shrieks of "Jessie, Jessie—Ayah, Ayah—" she retired to her bedroom and closed the door firmly. After some thought, she stripped and stared at her nude body in the long mirror, turning and twisting to inspect it from all angles. She combed out her rippling hair—fine, beautiful hair, the color of moonlight, which no man had ever seen in all its glory. Under the loose, smocklike

garments she habitually wore, her figure was good. A waist
any girl would envy, slender hips, rounded buttocks, long,
shapely legs. Small, pointed breasts. Her ankles and wrists
were slender, dainty. Hands, not so good. Rough, red. Skin
would be good with a little makeup—hide the blue circles
of exhaustion, the paleness of depression.

You're a fine-looking woman, Jessie, she told herself.
Time you went out and found yourself a man.

She sighed and started to plait her hair, coiling it on top
of her head, out of the way. Who was she fooling? No man
would take her, knowing he would have to take her mother
on as part of the deal. Oh God, why didn't the old harpy
die before it was too late?

"I deserve a man," Jessie hissed to her reflection. She
draped a silk counterpane around her and, putting a record
on the gramophone, wound it up. Then, as the music started,
she waltzed around, her arms out to an imaginary lover.
She closed her eyes and imagined him growing hard against
her. Farmyard images flashed through her mind, glistening
red, thrusting, spurting. Oh God, she wanted a man so bad,
so bad.

"Jessie, Jessie—Ayah, Ayah—"

"Damn it, will you never shut up?" she screamed.

"Jessie, Jessie—"

When it was obvious that Ayah was going to remain
where she was, Jessie sighed, dressed in her sackcloth and
ashes, and putting on the docile, patient look, wandered
into her mother's room.

"What do you want now?" she asked mildly.

"Read this." Her mother thrust a letter at her. "Came
by hand—wallah had to come into my room, couldn't get
anyone to answer the door."

"What is it?" said Jessie.

"I can't believe it. Not my James, he's been got at, he's
been tricked." Two red spots burned brightly in her mother's
cheeks. Her mouth quivered angrily.

Jessie took the letter and read it out loud.

*"Dear Mother,*

*I am sorry not to have written before, and to have stayed away so long. As you know, I was lent to the Indian Government to track and kill a man-eating tiger. At one point I had the honour to stay with a Colonel Armstrong, and by the time you read this, I will be married to his daughter."*

Mrs. Jameson exclaimed angrily, while Jessie said, "Good gracious!" She continued reading:

*"Miss Armstrong did me the honour of accepting my hand, and as her father is shortly retiring to England, we decided to tie the knot with no delay. We are honeymooning in Kashmir, and hope to see you upon our return.*

*Your dutiful son, James."*

Jessie stared at the note. "It's dated a month ago," she said. "Wonder why it took so long to reach us?" Suddenly she threw back her head and started laughing hysterically.

Mrs. Jameson frowned balefully. "Your brother trapped by a man-eater into an unsuitable marriage, and all you can do is laugh. Have you taken leave of your senses, girl?"

"He's not married to a tiger, Mother," Jessie gurgled.

Mrs. Jameson stared. "What? Are you crazy? Who said anything about being married to a tiger?"

"Well, he did go hunting a man-eater—and now you say a man-eater has trapped him."

"Ach!" Mrs. Jameson glared at Jessie irritably. "Don't be so foolish, girl. We have to talk to him—convince him he's made a mistake."

"He's married—it's too late for any discussions," Jessie cried impatiently. "Anyway—what's so unsuitable about Miss Armstrong? She's a colonel's daughter, probably got pots of money. Sounds as if James has done well for himself."

"He's my son—and some hussy has stolen him, that's

all I know," Mrs. Jameson exclaimed. "You act as if you don't care."

"Well, I don't care. He's old enough, and no loss to you or me. What has he ever done to help us? Took himself off as soon as he got a job, when he could have stayed here and helped with the bills—at least until he married. It would have made such a difference to our lives. He's just a selfish pig—if you ask me, Miss Armstrong is in for a big shock."

Mrs. Jameson stared at her. "You're daft, girl. I never took you to be mean and petty. Your brother married, and a fat lot you care. He was young, making his way in the world. As soon as he had settled, he would have helped us, I know it."

"Mother, your precious son is thirty-five years old! Doesn't that tell you something about all the help he was going to give us?"

"Well, he can't help us now, with a wife, so what's the use in discussing it? There's nothing for it—we must raffle the piano."

"Not the piano raffle again." Jessie started to giggle hysterically. "You can't. How many times have you raffled it already?"

"People forget quickly," Mrs. Jameson said disdainfully. "They're all fools."

"No, they're not. Why the piano—why not a chandelier, or a picture?"

"The piano," Mrs. Jameson said firmly. "Everyone wants a piano, and if they think they'll get one cheap, for the price of a raffle ticket, they'll jump at it."

"Well, we can't arrange the raffle now," Jessie said, resigning herself to the inevitable. "Soon be lunchtime. Wait till three—we'll go then."

"And I don't want you coming out with some remark about your brother's marriage," Mrs. Jameson said, frowning bitterly. "We'll break the news as if we are pleased and expected it. We won't give them a chance to gossip."

"There's nothing to gossip about," Jessie said maliciously. She sauntered out of the room. "Ayah," she called, "wash memsahib and fetch her lunch." She turned back. "Tell Ayah about James, and the whole community will know *before* lunch."

Laughing, she walked to the veranda, where she intended to eat her own meal in peace. So James was married, was he? What a joke. His new bride must be a weird one. Giggling, Jessie sank into a rattan chair. She doubted her brother even had a willie.

Mr. Edwards, from "The Cedars," stalked into his bungalow. He stood in the hall, his gold watch in his hands, after his bearer had respectfully divested him of his hat, overcoat, and stick.

"Where," he demanded, "where are the memsahib and the miss sahibs?"

"Bedroom, sahib. Missie Lizzie sick."

Recognising that in this instance, the mountain was unlikely to come to Mahomet, Mr. Edwards walked to his daughter's bedroom door and rapped on it sharply. Mrs. Edwards opened the door and, seeing her lord and master standing there with a thunderous face, came out, carefully closing the door behind her.

"I am truly sorry we did not follow you to church," she said.

"I take it you have a good excuse—or at least, the semblance of one?"

"Lizzie has taken bad. I have sent for the doctor."

Mr. Edwards frowned. He did not approve of illness. It was an inconvenience and a sign of weakness. He himself was never ill. "What's the matter with her, is it contagious?"

"I don't know, and I don't think so," answered his wife. She looked away, bit her lip, and after a moment added, "She thinks she is a bird."

"Off her food, eh?"

"No, that is not what I mean," his wife said. "I mean, she thinks she is a bird."

Mr. Edwards stared at her. "A bird? You mean a *bird*?" He flapped his elbows.

"That is exactly what I mean," replied Mrs. Edwards with composure. "She has tried to fly out of the window, pecks at her food, and a fine mess she has made. Then she insisted on bird-seed, took it away from the canary, and now she is standing on one foot, going tweet-tweet."

Mr. Edwards was thunderstruck. "Tweet-tweet? Are you sure that's what she's saying? Perhaps she is delirious."

"She may well be delirious, but tweet-tweet is all we're getting right now. However, she does respond when I whistle."

"Have you tried talking words to her?"

"Yes, but she acts as if she doesn't understand anything."

"When did all this come on?"

"She came back from school early yesterday with a migraine. Now this."

"Had a cousin once—third cousin twice removed, I think—anyway, he thought he was a bicycle," said Mr. Edwards reflectively. "Of course, he got removed completely in the end; they carted him off to a sanitorium."

"Well, if we don't do something about this, they may have to cart Lizzie off," Mrs. Edwards said firmly.

"Good God—d'you think she's mad?"

"Possibly," said his wife. "And it doesn't run in my family, that much is now obvious." She returned to the room, closing the door behind her.

Mr. Edwards walked slowly up and down, his hands clasped behind his back. Lizzie, his bright, intelligent girl—hadn't she obtained her teaching certificate? Wasn't she now teaching at the Misses Anderton's school? Although there was no real need for her to work at all, he had plenty of money. His wife was mistaken. Making up his mind, he strode purposefully into Lizzie's room without knocking.

"Good morning, Lizzie," he began.

"Tweet," she said brightly, flapping her arms and hopping around her room. "Tweet-tweet."

"Lizzie, enough of this nonsense. If this is a joke, it's gone far enough."

"Tweet," responded Lizzie, tucking her head under an arm and balancing on one foot. A "tweet" followed Mr. Edwards as he walked to the door.

"I will discuss it with the doctor when he has seen her," he said with dignity.

In his study, Mr. Edwards stared moodily out of the window, then rang for a chota-peg. When it came, he hesitated as he was about to add soda to the glass. No, strong drink was called for, for once in his life. He tossed back the whisky and poured another.

I am a godly man, he thought morosely. I have not sinned, I attend church regularly. I have taught my family to respect God. I am not a drunk. I do not gamble with money, nor lust after women, even when they are very beautiful and absolutely flaunt themselves at me. I am just with my workers, punishing only where merited. I am not as other men—so it will be all right.

He found *The News of the World* where he had concealed it that morning before church, and started reading. It was a sensational newspaper, a scandal-rag, and one that his family was not permitted to read. It could not have been anything shocking she had read that had made Lizzie go weird, he reflected. He was very careful about that; she had been brought up to be a good, wholesome girl.

When Dr. Bannerjee came in to talk to him, he did not ask him to sit down, it was not done. "Well," he said, folding the newspaper and putting it under the cushion of his chair, "she's all right, isn't she—be better tomorrow, eh?"

"I'm afraid not," said Dr. Bannerjee. "Her mind has gone."

"Gone? What's gone can come back, can't it?" Mr. Edwards blustered.

"Sometimes," the doctor conceded.

"Well, then—make sure Lizzie's mind comes back. Shouldn't be too difficult—she's a bright gal."

"I don't think you understand," the doctor said. "Mental illness is very hard to diagnose and cure. In fact, Miss Lizzie might become worse."

"Worse? What can be worse than thinking you are a bird?" Mr. Edwards snorted. "Or do you mean she might get dangerous?"

"No, I don't think she'll become dangerous. I meant she might change her mind—it might take another form, her delusion. I have arranged for a nurse. We have her in bed, and she has been sedated. You don't want her wandering about in her state."

"Why me?" Mr. Edwards demanded pathetically. "Why does such a thing have to happen to me? I am an elder of the church."

Dr. Bannerjee looked at him. "You ask me that—don't you know?"

"No," said Mr. Edwards. "God is probably testing me; there are many historic precedences. It will pass."

Dr. Bannerjee shrugged and left the house.

Mr. Edwards poured another drink and stood looking out the window while he drank it. Why a bird? he asked himself. An angel, I could understand, but a bird! Now Aunt Matilda was no problem. Thought she was a teapot, never moved, never troubled anyone, none of this flying-out-the-window nonsense and going "tweet." All Aunt Matilda ever requested visitors to do was to pour her out, and that she did only once. Very upset, of course, when they declined, but after that, she more or less left 'em alone. Retreated back down her spout and settled for just being a teapot.

His wife appeared. "What are we going to do?" she demanded.

"Do?" repeated Mr. Edwards.

"Yes—we can't hide her condition for long; the servants will gossip. Then there is the school. We will have to tell them."

"I don't know what you mean by gossip. People get ill, nothing earth-shattering about that. I dare say in a week or so Lizzie will be back at school, teaching."

His wife sighed. "Lizzie can never go back," she said

slowly, as if explaining matters to a child. "Lizzie will become worse, like Aunt Matilda."

"Just thinking of Aunt Matilda," Mr. Edwards confessed.

"You should have thought of Aunt Matilda before you got married and had a family," Mrs. Edwards said. "Especially in view of the cousin who was a bicycle—you never told me about him."

"What are you trying to say?"

"Inherited madness. It is perfectly obvious that it runs in your family—did it never dawn on you?"

Mr. Edwards stared at her.

"I would still have married you, I loved you—but it was criminal to have had children—to have passed it on to them. And now Claire is expecting. How can we tell her?"

"But I didn't do anything wrong," Mr. Edwards said pathetically. "I never realised—"

"It was criminal of you not to have told me," Mrs. Edwards repeated. "*I* would have realised. You are not a stupid man, Arthur, but you are like most pompously moral men—arrogant. I hope you understand now that there is a taint in your family that we have to deal with for the sake of future generations."

"What must we do?"

"Well, to start with, we can't let Claire see Lizzie in this state. In her condition, it would cause all kinds of problems. Tell her Lizzie has German measles. That will keep her away for a while, and get Sonny and Edna here at once. We must have a family conference."

Sonny Edwards and his wife, Claire, were in the sitting room of their comfortable bungalow before lunch. Sonny—tall, blond, blue-eyed—worked for the Railway in some supervisory capacity in the workshops. Not because he was particularly bright, but because he was a damned good sportsman and his fairness looked good when representing the Railway against the Army or the Civil Service at cricket or polo. He knew he would never have to work hard at anything, for one day he would inherit pots of money from his father. Claire (rounded, pretty, with the typical Welsh colouring of dark, curly hair, large violet eyes, and a peachy complexion inherited from her mother, Mrs. Darsi Jones) lay back on a sofa, feeling nauseous in her third month. She wanted to lie quietly in her room with a damp towel on her forehead, but Sonny was like his father. He did not acknowledge weakness. She met her brother-in-law's eyes and flushed.

Joseph had distinctive features and rich, auburn hair. Big, bearlike, he was nothing like her husband. When the baby was born, suppose it looked like Joseph? Would people comment? Would Sonny guess?

Joseph Sherman was Edna's husband. People couldn't understand why; Claire couldn't understand why. He was gentle, courteous. Sonny's sister, Edna, was enormous, not so much in person (Claire thought she was fat) as in presence. Loud, vulgar, mannish, she dominated any room with her strident laugh and double entendres.

Not a lady, was Claire's verdict, turning her eyes again towards Joseph. Her expression softened. What on earth had he seen in Edna? She couldn't ever have been pretty. Why hadn't he seen Claire first? Oh, what a mess everything was.

Sonny was mixing drinks while Edna shrieked across the room at him, recounting one of the disgusting jokes she had picked up at the bar of the Tobacco Factory Club.

She was rolling around, heaving with laughter, when a beaver arrived with two letters on a silver salver. He bowed to Sonny.

"Wants an answer, sahib," said the bearer, moving on to present Edna with the salver. She took the second letter, looking apprehensive.

Sonny ripped his letter open. "Lord, it's a summons from the Old Man. Must see me urgently, Lizzie is ill."

Claire made to get up. "Oh, poor Lizzie. I hope it's not serious."

"Father says you are not to come," read Sonny. "He says it's infectious, not safe in your condition."

Relieved, Claire sat down. "What about lunch—shall we wait for you?"

"No—you and Joseph go ahead and eat—we'll probably be back soon."

"We?" Claire asked.

"Wants to see Edna, too."

"But Maisie is there, and your mother—surely you don't both need to go?" Claire said, her heart singing. Alone with Joseph, just the two of them. Lunch, a view of the hills, lingering glances; they could pretend it was like that all the time.

Edna crumpled her letter, her face very white. "Damn, damn, damn," she said viciously.

"Steady on, old girl—" said Joseph. "Can't be as bad as all that—"

"I've been expecting something like this for years," Edna said bitterly. "Mother gave me a hint or two—"

"What on earth?" asked Sonny.

"You'll soon see," Edna replied, her eyes very hard.


As the lunch hour approached outside the Railway store-cum-pub, groups of men and the odd, no-good, brazen woman could be seen chatting. Inside was a rumbling of voices and an occasional burst of song over the jangling notes of an upright piano.

Chatterjee, the manager, could be heard anxiously announcing, "Sahibs, time to go. Mems when they come shopping will be blaming me for cold lunch, burnt lunch, and all sorts of happenings. My wife, she will be leaving me or withholding favours, never have she proper mealtime. Sahibs, half an hour gone closing time."

In dribs and drabs, prodded by Chatterjee, the late drinkers reeled out. Jim Dale, fitter and gardener, scratched his head.

"What you push me out for?" he demanded, trying to go back in.

"If Chatterjee doesn't close lunchtime, how can he open evening, eh?" Chatterjee reasoned.

Jim Dale sat on the step and leaned against the closed door. "I'm staying," he said.

His friends tried to drag him up. "C'mon, Jimmy, you'll be for it if you're found in the ditch again."

Les Topping, recently appointed Secretary of the Institute, approached. "Take him to Tom Knowles, he'll handle him."

Les Topping, a faultlessly turned out dream, polished and burnished, superb manners, superb dancer; envied by men, adored by women, never-put-a-foot-wrong Topping.

"Good old Tom, he'll fix me up, always got a drop of the right stuff," Jim muttered, staggering to his feet but falling over the step.

Topping signalled a passing refuse cart, "Ho! Wallah!"

"I'm not going on that," Jim protested as his friends picked him up and swung him—one-two-three—through the air onto the rubbish.

"One rupee. Take sahib to Hostel, care of Knowles sahib," Topping directed, handing over a coin.

"Very good, sahib." The cart lumbered off, pulled by a buffalo.

Topping returned briskly to the remaining group. "Don't forget, main hall, we're giving out the parts for the musical— *Belle of New York*—six o'clock on the dot. Let your neighbours know. Cheerio." He smiled pleasantly and walked off.

"Funny fellow," said one, gazing after him. "Can't make him out—always so damned perfect. It ain't natural."

"We can't all be rotters, can we?" returned another.

At the Hostel, Mr. Knowles and Solomon were relaxing for a brief moment after the last course of the last sitting.

"Very good effort, Solomon. Papworth sahib was very impressed. I must say, you have worked wonders with the bearers; they would be good enough for the Viceroy."

Solomon beamed. "Bloody good show, sahib. Solomon tell them one bearer unclean, no tips at Nautch. All bearers want to go Nautch—very fine Railway Apprentices' Ball."

"Of course," said Mr. Knowles. "Let's see—that's on Saturday week. Means a trip to Calcutta, what? We'll have to see the Committee and get the orders. You'll want to come, won't you?"

"Sahib, only Solomon can help, who else?" He beamed, remembering the tips of previous years. Chandhi would then realise what a king amongst men she had. Ayee, she would show much respect. Sipping some lemonade, he smiled at the images such respect conjured up.

Mr. Knowles moved off to the kitchen. It always paid to scatter praise where it was due, made people happy.

"Charlie," he said, "that roast beef was excellent. The best Papworth sahib has tasted outside of England. Told me so himself."

Charlie, sharpening his knife, grinned. "Only Charlie can do it, sahib. He jump on it, two feet, march march. Very good. Then he stretch it and beat it with sticks. Only the flesh of a mule could put up with such treatment."

"Good Lord, I hope your feet were clean."

"Very clean, sahib, cleaner than floor. But good thing Apprentice sahibs have digestion of old goats. Eating mule, buff'lo, no good."

"What about Papworth sahib's digestion—I don't want him to get a belly-ache."

"Papworth sahib great white god, gods no have belly-ache, only ordinary white sahibs and niggers." Charlie smiled proudly. "If sahib pleased, then Charlie happy."

Mr. Knowles returned to his bungalow for lunch.

"Heavens!" he exclaimed as he opened the door. "What on earth is that smell—haven't the commodes been emptied, or is it the drains again?"

His wife pointed to the sitting room. "It's him, that Dale chappie. Asleep in your chair."

Mr. Knowles walked to the door and looked in. "Good God! How did he get there?"

Mrs. Knowles shrugged. "I don't know. I was supervising the cook in the kitchen."

Jim Dale was sprawled out, snoring; old food clung to his hair, and various messes stuck to his clothes. He had trailed disgusting items in his wake.

The house bearer entered and bowed. "Sahib, mem, Topping sahib sent Dale sahib to you. In refuse cart he came; I gave wallah one rupee. Memsahib busy in kitchen."

Baffled, Mr. and Mrs. Knowles stared at Jim Dale. "Les Topping sent him in a refuse cart? Very odd," said Mr. Knowles. "Well, don't worry about it—send the mali along, and the sweeper."

"Very good, sahib."

When the two lower servants arrived, they carried the leather chair complete with Jim Dale into the back yard.

"Mali, turn the hose on him, clean off all the filth— you, sweeper, sweep it all into the drain," Mr. Knowles directed. Hiding a grin, Mrs. Knowles returned to the house to change for lunch. Her church garments were too stuffy, too tight; she enjoyed a good meal and a nice long nap after, and a loose, smocklike gown accommodated both activities in a greater degree of comfort.

Like little boys, the sweeper and the mali set to work with a will, spraying jets of water into Jim Dale's nose and mouth, loving the white sahib's howls and struggles. His clothes were stripped off and given to the dhobi-wallah for washing; he was towelled dry and pushed into one of Mr. Knowles' capacious suits.

Placidly, Mr. and Mrs. Knowles ate their meal, ignoring the pantomime in the back yard.

Mr. Knowles lit a cigar and strolled out. Exhausted, looking wretched, Dale was draped in a hammock. "Better send for his daughter," Mr. Knowles instructed the bearer. "She'll know what to do with him now."

"Oh God, I need a drink," Dale muttered.

*       *       *

Mr. Knowles and Mrs. Knowles lay on their bed, relaxing.

"Another hundred apprentices arriving by the three-thirty train," Mrs. Knowles said sleepily.

Mr. Knowles grunted.

"How did the lunch go?" Mrs. Knowles wanted to know.

"Papworth was most gracious. Actually asked us to Officers' Club Night as his guests. Wants to meet Mary, said his wife was most impressed with her. News to me Mary mixes in such elevated circles."

"We are not going," said his wife firmly. "I know Papworth and his dirty weekends with young gels. He noticed her in church—you know how cheeky she is. Winked at him. It got him going, the old goat."

"You women," said Mr. Knowles. There was a silence. "So Papworth has dirty weekends, does he? Beats me how you get all the scandal."

"Women with daughters make it their business to know what's what," Mrs. Knowles said sedately. "By the way, you'd better watch Philip. I don't like him hanging about the servants' quarters, singing those silly songs. The men don't like it, and we can't afford servant trouble."

"Oh, Philip is harmless, the men know that. He's just a natural mimic."

"I don't know, walking about, singing about his larve, larve. Gives the women ideas. But we'll see. What I don't understand is Les Topping's behaviour. What have you done to him?"

"Nothing, I hardly ever see him except at the committee meetings. Seems a nice enough chap, mixes with all the right people."

"Well, there's nothing very nice about putting Jim Dale in a rubbish cart, sending him here, and making us pay for the honour, that's all I can say. There has to be a reason—you'll see."

"Go to sleep, Mother. Soon be time to be thinking about all those new apprentices and dinner."

\*       \*       \*

$M$rs. Ray lay on a chaise-longue in her lounge, clad in a gauze negligee. She was fuming. An empty green gin bottle stood on the brass table next to her.

"That George O'Leary," she muttered. "I won't be treated as a cast-off, he won't get rid of me that easily, oh, no. He'll find he can't just pick me up and toss me aside for a pasty-faced schoolgirl." She rang a small handbell. "What has she got? No dress sense, no figure, nothing. He'll be robbing cradles next." She rang the bell furiously.

Her husband, Dr. Ray, came into the room, a slight, mild-mannered man with a charming smile. "On your own?" he enquired.

"Damned fool—is it a crowd you can see? Give me a drink—anything, but not a bloody cup-of-tea, the stunt you usually pull."

He picked up the gin bottle. "It's empty."

"Of course it's empty—if it were full would I ask you to get me a drink?" Angrily she thumped a cushion. "This place stifles me. Drab, drab, drab. All the women ever talk about are babies and more babies, their boring husbands, and their endless problems with their servants."

"If you had a baby of your own, you would not think their conversation boring."

"Spare me! We're not going through that again, are we?"

"No," he said mildly. "I believe I understand your feelings on that subject well enough. But if you tried to see things from other people's point of view, you'd understand their interests better."

"God, you're a pompous ass, Jeremy. Where's that drink?"

Dr. Ray started to pour out a drink at a cabinet on the far side of the room.

"Don't bother to pour it, just bring me the bottle," she demanded. "You didn't tell me when you dragged me here what it would be like. Stupid, ignorant people! The duller they are, the dowdier they are, the more airs they give them-

selves. What would they be like in London? In Paris? Eh,
you tell me that?"

Dr. Ray handed her the unopened bottle. "Boyfriend
trouble?" he enquired pleasantly.

"A lot you care. Should I need boyfriends if you were
more than half a man? If I had a dozen boyfriends, what
would you do? Leave me? Throw me out? Huh! You wouldn't
have the guts. That precious job means more to you than
my feelings. You're a cold fish, Jeremy. Like everyone else
here. Dead, the lot of you are, dead, from the bottom of
your old school ties down. If the whole place caved in it
wouldn't make a scrap of difference to the world."

Dr. Ray stared at her silently.

The bearer appeared. "Memsahib Jameson at the door."

"Tell her to sod off!" screamed Mrs. Ray. "I've had
enough of memsahibs to last me a lifetime!"

Dr. Ray made for the door. "I'll see to it," he said, and
left the room.

Jessie Jameson stood, white-faced and sick-looking, on
the doorstep. Her mother, in her wheelchair, was at the
bottom of the steps, arrayed in a vast black dress, regal like
Queen Victoria.

Jessie was turning to go. She had heard the scream.
"I'm so sorry to disturb you. It was not important."

Mrs. Jameson shook a book of raffle-tickets at arm's
length. "Ask him to take some—ask him," she called out.

Jessie backed away, hunching her shoulders, a look of
disgust, of degradation, pinching her features. Her mouth
had a faint bluish tinge. "It's nothing, really," she stam-
mered. "Excuse me." She hastened down the steps and
clutched at the handles of the wheelchair.

Dr. Ray followed her, his heart melting at her blind,
empty expression. "Can I help?"

Mrs. Jameson craned her neck around, beaming. "Raffle
tickets for a piano, only a rupee each." She waved the book
cheerily.

Jessie grabbed the book. "Mother! Stop it!"

"But he's going to buy some, dear."

"Mother!" Jessie started to sob with vexation and shame.

"Miss Jameson, please don't. It's all right." Dr. Ray was there, taking the handles from her unresisting fingers. "Where to?"

"It's all right," sobbed Jessie. "I can manage."

"But I'm not going to let you." Her vulnerable air touched his Socratean soul. The brittle void at his wife's centre would never be satisfied by anything he had to offer. "This chair is far too heavy for you to push about these roads. Where to?"

"Home," Jessie murmured.

"Home it is," he said, smiling down at her.

"We can't go home, we haven't sold any tickets yet," objected Mrs. Jameson. "Unless Dr. Ray intends to buy them all."

"By all means," Dr. Ray said equably, causing Jessie's mouth to fall open with shock. "I want the lot," he added.

Inside the bungalow, Mrs. Ray summoned the bearer and demanded to know where her husband was when he had not reappeared after ten minutes.

"Sahib gone home with Miss Sahib Jameson."

Mrs. Ray petulantly splashed some gin into her glass. "What's wrong with everyone—is everyone mad?" she muttered. "Another whey-faced bag."

Her negligee slipped open. The bearer fastened his eyes on the taut rosy nipples thus exposed, on the curving, slender throat thrown back to swallow the gin, on the flaming halo of hennaed hair. His eyes grew hot. With an effort he backed away, first hitting the wall, before clutching for the door handle and tumbling through.

The three-thirty p.m. Loop Line train was full. In a first-class compartment were four hopeful Special Grade apprentices, a clergyman, and a bird of paradise.

Of the young men, two, Andrew and Robert McIntosh, were dissimilar twins; the other two, looking alike, were not related. Freddy Payne was a first-class runner and hurdler;

John Brown, a boxer. Within an hour of meeting they had sworn eternal friendship, and were now playing cards.

The clergyman seemed preoccupied. He had spent almost the entire journey sitting by a window, gazing out, muttering to himself and taking delicate, old-maidish sips from a leather bottle. He leaned forward suddenly. "Any of you boys know J.M.P.?"

Surprised, they looked up from their game and shook their heads.

"You, madam?" he asked.

The bird of paradise lit a cigarette. The smoke trailed through the veil of her feathered cloche. Her lipstick stained the end of the cigarette with a scarlet circle.

"No," she said finally. "I don't know J.M.P. Never been there—got someone there, though. Someone close."

"From Calcutta, madam?"

"Oh no! Good heavens, no!" she said untruthfully. "I was born in Scotland. I'm Scotch. Mimosa McIntosh, that's me."

"Och, that's a coincidence," Andrew said with a marked accent. "McIntosh, that's our name, too. An' which parrt o' Scotland are you frae, Miss McIntosh?"

"I really can't remember. I said I was born there, not lived there," Mimosa replied, hurriedly dragging on her cigarette.

Andrew hid a grin. "Bet she wishes she'd chosen another name," he murmured to his brother under the sound of the train.

"Scotch. Always thought that was a drink," Robert grinned.

Fresh from Blighty, intoxicated to the point of delirium with the heady brew of India, John Brown grew giddy watching Mimosa sucking at her cigarette. He started to fantasize, longing to place something rather larger than a slim white tube between the glossy red lips.

Unaware of the use to which her tumescent mouth was being put, Mimosa had been brooding. "Anyway, I'm not McIntosh any more," she announced from her corner. "Been married six months. Mrs. Bertram Papworth, that's me."

"Reverend Morgan Morgan, late of the Welsh Guards," suddenly introduced the clergyman. "Going to J.M.P. to recuperate. It's ill I've been."

"Ill?" Andrew muttered, watching the preacher take another sip. "He's absolutely blotto."

The train passed through a tunnel. Mimosa was reflected in the window, a paler version of her brilliant self. The Reverend Morgan Morgan stared, transfixed.

"Oh, Avril, Avril, how long it's been. Wherever I go, it's your face I see." He stroked the dusty pane with a trembling hand. "Oh, Avril, I have searched for you in the wind, I have looked for you in the rain. Oh, Avril, come in, come in."

"Poor man," said Mimosa. She shaped her lips into a kiss and gazed into Morgan Morgan's reflected eyes.

"Avril—Avril my love!" Morgan Morgan glued his lips to the glass.

"Good Lord, don't do that," said Freddy Payne to Mimosa. "You'll have him disrobed in a minute."

"Defrocked, more likely," Robert suggested.

"Poor man," Mimosa repeated. "He must have loved his Avril very much. He deserves a little encouragement."

As soon as the Reverend unglued his lips and moved back to smile mistly at his Avril, Mimosa gave him a little wave and shaped another kiss. Almost before the motion was made, Morgan Morgan fell back hungrily upon the glass.

Mimosa shied back. "It's weird. I feel as if he's actually making love to me."

John Brown suddenly spoke. "Why don't you let him, then? Give him a thrill."

Mimosa was not insulted. "You're too young to know what it's like to have loved someone for years and years. We don't know how much he's suffered. We sing about love, but what is it but pain and suffering? Have you ever seen happy people in love?"

The four young men looked at each other, somewhat

startled by this turn in the conversation. It was far removed from a boisterous game of snap.

Freddy Payne shrugged. "Don't know, ma'am. Had crushes and fancied various girls, I suppose—but love? Not guilty."

"Why do you say that?" asked Mimosa. "Why guilty? Is love a sin?"

Andrew burst into song. "'I'm guilty. . . .' You heard it? It's by that new crooner whatsisname. Everyone is crazy about him."

"Let's all sing it, it's one of my favourites," Mimosa cried enthusiastically. She smiled at them.

"Gosh, how pretty you look when you smile," Freddy said impetuously. "Makes you look a lot younger, too. Why, you're probably about our age."

"I'm twenty-two, bet you're just eighteen, maybe younger," Mimosa replied, then started singing, "I'm guilty . . . of love . . . guilty. . . ." Her voice was low and husky.

Transfixed, the Reverend Morgan Morgan was gazing into the window. They were out of the tunnel, and Mimosa's reflected image was very faint, just a hint that she was there at all.

"Avril, Avril, don't go—I hear your voice," he cried, tears running down his cheeks. He opened his mouth and an incredible sound poured out, glorious, vibrant, the sound of Wales.

The other five in the carriage sat listening, spellbound. As the last note died away, Reverend Morgan Morgan fell back against the squabs, his mouth open, snoring.

Mimosa sighed. "That's the most beautiful thing I ever heard. Pity it was in a foreign language."

"It was Welsh," Robert explained. "A hymn, I dare say. They sing lots of hymns in Wales. In fact, they sing a lot of anything in Wales."

The Reverend Morgan Morgan was still sleeping soundly and loudly, despite all efforts to rouse him, when the train drew into the station. As the train shuddered to a halt, Freddy leapt off and called to a guard. Within moments two porters and a stretcher arrived, and the sad Welshman was carried off to hospital.

"Bet he'll be surprised when he wakes up and finds himself there," Freddy said, grinning.

"What did you tell them?" Mimosa asked.

"That he had suddenly taken ill," Freddy shrugged.

"Suddenly taken drunk, more like it," Robert started to say when he broke off, his mouth open. He was staring up the platform to where Mary Knowles was waiting patiently to one side as her father was directing the Ordinary Apprentices to the Hostel.

"Will you look at that?" he breathed. "Have you ever seen anything more gorgeous?"

"Probably married with three kids," said Andrew.

"She can't be—because she is going to marry me," Robert declared reverently. "I knew there was a reason for coming all this way."


The Maharajah had a passion for motor-cars. After lunch, he sent a canary-yellow Citroën with a liveried driver to collect Jane. Under her father's ever-watchful eyes, she climbed in, closely followed by her Ayah, who carried Jane's music case. The Sergeant-Major would have preferred it if his wife also accompanied Jane, but Mrs. Barhill said she felt foolish sitting around the palace twiddling her thumbs— and what possible mischief could Jane get into whilst giving piano lessons to three small princesses?

"Never know with these wogs," Sergeant-Major Barhill muttered darkly, but not being able to find a more tangible reason to refuse the Maharajah's request, and not willing to insult him, he was forced to let Jane go with his usual rejoinder to "watch it."

The car sped away down Prince's Road, into King's Road, and then turned out of town on the Grand Trunk Road.

Sugar cane and pineapples grew in the fields, and the native workers stopped to watch the car passing, salaaming. A boy drove two water buffalo along, the tiny stick with which he urged them looking ridiculously puny. Groves of trees, limes and mangoes, stood in clumps by the sides of the road. Small shrines, bright with red and orange flowers, were in their shadowed depths. Some of these groves—the ones with shrines—had been the sites of ritual strangulation in the past and were known as *bele*. The secret cult of Thuggee was all but eradicated, but years earlier, initiated members had taken their silken ropes and with them strangled travellers in their terrible worship of Kali, goddess of blood and death.

They reached the palace. The gold-leaf and turquoise decoration of the white domes made intricate and beautiful designs. The glistening marble was fretted into fragile screens around the courtyards where fountains made rainbow sprays and golden carp darted. Jane grimaced as she looked down at her severe dress, at such odds with so much luxury and grace. With a quick gesture she pulled the restraining pin out of the neckline, and made her way to the music room.

The little girls came running to greet her, long black pigtails swinging. They were dressed in simple silk tunics, each a different colour, pink and blue and yellow, and white silk pantaloons.

"Missie Jane, Missie Jane—"

Laughing and chattering like charming birds, they pulled her towards the two splendid concert grands under the crystal chandeliers.

In an adjoining room, a game of poker had been going on all night. Rich jewels and American dollars were strewn in heaps over the table. The Maharajah had just lost his favorite car, a Stutz Bearcat, to MacNamara, one of his oldest friends from his Oxford days, and was enjoying himself enormously.

After Oxford, MacNamara, the scion of an impoverished Irish family, had gone on to become a brilliant actor.

A purist, he had scorned the many lures cast in his direction to act in films; but now, on a visit to the Maharajah, had been tracked down by Von Stroginski, a big-shot director from Hollywood, and the movie mogul, Goldfinch. Von Stroginski wanted MacNamara, and what he wanted, he ruthlessly pursued.

Von Stroginski suddenly flung himself back in his chair. He pointed at Goldfinch; Prussian and Jew, these two had maintained a running battle for years. "I ain't playing no more viz zat bum—he cheats."

"Who cheats?" yelled Goldfinch. "What about that game of craps on the boat? Who cheated there, huh?"

MacNamara smiled cynically. "Why don't you fight it out like men?"

Von Stroginski jumped up excitedly and strode around the table, cracking the whip without which he never moved. "A duel, *hein*? *Ja*—let's haf a duel."

Goldfinch was taken aback. "Ya mean a shoot-out?"

"No—Marquess of Queensbury rules," MacNamara replied languidly.

"Marquess of who?" said Von Stroginski.

"Wonderful idea, dear chap," cried the Maharajah. "Let us proceed to the gymnasium."

"I ain't boxing that punk," said Goldfinch. "He'll probably keel over with a heart-attack and I'll get the blame. No sir, include me out."

"You are a coward, sir!" Von Stroginski exclaimed, slashing the air with his whip.

"Shove it, kraut," snarled Goldfinch.

"Gentlemen, gentlemen," cried the Maharajah jovially, "perhaps we are all tired. Un *petit* adjournment is called for, *n'est-ce pas*?"

Von Stroginski laughed and slapped Goldfinch on the back with the stock of his whip. "We didn't come to India to fight, *hein*, Goldfinch?"

"Damn right," said Goldfinch, eyeing the whip warily.

"No sir, we came to get you, MacNamara. Vat about it, *hein*? You vill be ze star of my new picture?"

MacNamara shook his head. "I think not," he said.

"I vill play you for it," said Von Stroginski in a flash of pure inspiration. "You vin, I vill give you a million dollars. You lose, you return to Hollywood viz me, three-year contract, top salary, all za trimmings, what ya say?"

Coolly MacNamara nodded. He had never been known to refuse a bet. "But I choose the game," he said.

"I vill not fight you," Von Stroginski warned. "None of zat Marquess of whatzit bullshit."

MacNamara smiled faintly and, opening his wallet, extracted a large white English five-pound note. He dipped his finger in some Scotch and carefully ran it around the rim of an empty glass. Then he placed the fiver over the top of the glass, watching the suction of the liquid making a tight seal. In the center of the taut note he placed a silver rupee. The others looked perplexed.

"Gentlemen, when I was in the desert with Lawrence, there wasn't much for a chap to do to amuse himself. We used to play a little game to see who paid for the next bottle or the next round of drinks."

"My dear chap, I didn't know you were in the desert with Lawrence of Arabia," said the Maharajah.

MacNamara raised his eyebrows. "Figuratively speaking, old chap." He picked up a glowing cheroot from the ashtray by his side. "If you light up, Stroggy, I'll explain," he said.

Suspiciously, Von Stroginski lighted a cigar, while the Maharajah beamed with delight. "Jolly good show," he said.

MacNamara proceeded to explain that they would each burn a hole in turn in the five-pound note. The one who finally caused the coin to fall into the tumbler was the loser.

"Hey, I like it," Von Stroginski exclaimed, after carefully considering where the catch was and deciding the game was on the level.

Total silence. The air was wreathed in smoke. MacNamara and Von Stroginski were looking intently at the glass; the Maharajah and Goldfinch had moved in closer. The fiver was full of holes, there was scarcely space for a glowing tip to be placed. Suddenly the coin fell with an electrifying tinkle.

Von Stroginski leapt to his feet. "I vin, I vin! Got you, Mac!"

MacNamara inclined his head. "For three years," he agreed quietly.

The Maharajah rubbed his hands. "Jolly good show. Anyone for poker, gentlemen?"

MacNamara rose. "Count me out of this hand. I need to stretch my legs." He walked across the room, a tall, elegant figure in a black dinner jacket, and passed through the windows into the lush verdure of the courtyard. He could hear music and childish laughter.

Jane was playing and singing an amusing song she had made up for the princesses, and they were clapping their hands with delight, trying to learn the words.

Riveted, MacNamara stood outside the open windows of the music room and absorbed Jane's lovely profile, noting her ravishing auburn hair, so at odds with her dowdy, schoolmarmish dress. Without moving, he watched for several minutes, before pulling himself together with an effort and moving away.

"No ties, MacNamara," he told himself. "You promised yourself no ties."

When he went back later for another look, irresistibly drawn by Jane's rare beauty, she had gone.

The Institute. Three pairs of imposing, ornamental iron gates; smooth watered lawns, emerald green always; beds full of gladioli, canna lillies, azaleas. Standard roses, all colours. Pools with water-lotus, golden carp. Peacock plumes, bulbuls, budgerigars, coral flamingos. Striped awnings, very handsome, like Monte Carlo. Sweeping marble stairs, so lovely will look the ladies in their ball gowns. Very fine place was the Institute on the outside.

Interior, equally grand. Ballroom for dancing, theatre for bioscope and dramatic art. Dressing rooms. Well-stocked bar run by Babu, good at listening and keeping mouth shut. Library, lots of books. Little Maisie Edwards ran the library; people didn't know yet that her sister was a bird.

Next to the library was a reading room, with cane tables and chairs, lots of palm trees in big pots. It was a busy room. Here, the English magazines and newspapers arrived every week, only six weeks old, and were much sought after for the latest fashions, the latest films and plays, the continuation of exciting serials, and for the children's "Pip, Squeak, and Wilfred." "No Pip and Squeak for you" was a devastating threat by exasperated parents.

No women (unless on a committee) or children were allowed past the reading room to the Secretary's office or the committee rooms. Les Topping's suite of rooms was above the library and reading room, but it was a mystery to most people where the stairway was concealed. Very private person was Les Topping.

Behind the offices were the tennis courts, scene of great passion, start of many romances and some affairs. The red-brick Victorian swimming baths were segregated—schedule for men, schedule for women pinned up on the door. Boy children swam with the women. Non-whites didn't swim at all.

That evening, there were two committee meetings. One for the Apprentices' Ball, one of the grand occasions of the year. People came from every corner of the East Indian Railway to attend it, fighting for tickets, frantic when they were left out. The Railway gave a grant of thirty thousand rupees for refreshments and decorations, and it was all perfectly splendid. The other committee was Les Topping's special project, *The Belle of New York*, which he hoped to direct and even to take on tour. Naturally, he kept most of this to himself; people had a habit of being scornful of ambition.

Mr. Nightingale, Mr. Knowles, Mrs. Knowles, Mr. Grundy, Babu, five apprentices (one for each year), and Les Topping (a newcomer to their ranks who had to prove himself) made up the Ball committee.

Mr. Grundy, principal of the Technical College, was not

prepared to be agreeable. He screwed up his nose and mouth. "Rather bad management on your part, old chap. Hear you have a drama committee meeting. Not even you can be in two places at one time."

Topping nodded. "That's right, sir. But you know how the ladies are. By the time they arrive I dare say *our* meeting will be over."

"Don't intend rushing us, do you? Not bally racehorses, what?"

"No, sir. I've drawn up an agenda. We should cover everything in an hour."

"Well, get on with it, on with it." Mr. Grundy shifted in his chair and glared at the committee. "If we have to gallop through because of bad organization, better use the little time we've been allowed. What's first?"

"The band," announced Topping.

"What about the band we had last year?" suggested Mr. Knowles. "Everyone had a good time."

"As I understand it, it was rather old-fashioned. The younger generation want something modern; after all," Topping smiled at the apprentices, "this is the Apprentices' Ball."

"Hear, hear!" The apprentices thumped the table vigorously.

"Good," said Topping, moving on to the next item on his agenda. "Printing of the programs. I have approached the Tobacco Factory printing works—I have some contacts there—" He smiled modestly. "They can do it for a good price."

"Hey, hold on," said Mr. Nightingale, accountant. "Why should we pay for printing? Our workshop printers have always done it for nothing."

"And while we're about it, we haven't agreed on the band," said Mr. Grundy. "Who have you got in mind?"

"The Woody Woodman Quartet—they're a sensation."

"I know most of the decent bands in Calcutta—never heard of Woody Whatsit," declared Mr. Grundy.

"I'm not surprised, sir. They're from New Delhi."

Mr. Grundy glared. "I think we will stick to the band we had last year. They were good, they were inexpensive, and my wife liked them."

"What about catering?" Mrs. Knowles wanted to know. "Same as last year?"

"I have discussed catering with Blumes—" Topping began.

"Blumes? But we always do the catering," protested Mrs. Knowles. "No-one has ever complained before."

"Blumes are very cheap. I was looking through the accounts for last year, and—" started Topping.

"What are you suggesting?" said Mr. Knowles.

"Why, sir, nothing. It was just that the profit margin on your catering—"

Mr. Knowles stood up. "Profit margin? There is no profit margin. My wife and I and the Hostel staff do it for nothing—the bills are all sent to the committee." He glared at Les Topping. "And while we're about it, I didn't appreciate that practical joke you pulled on us this afternoon. Good day." He bowed to Mr. Grundy and Mr. Nightingale, and, followed by his startled wife, stalked out.

Looking somewhat uncertain, Topping ploughed bravely on. "Accommodation for out-of-town guests. I see they are usually put up by Railway families. Takes a lot of organization. I propose that we erect tents on the Maidan—separate tents for women and men—"

"Good God, man! Have you entirely taken leave of your senses? What do you propose our visitors do for toilets? Take lotahs and squat by the side of the road?"

After a few more minutes, the meeting erupted into a full-scale argument between all parties. A few more minutes and it broke up. As Mr. Grundy got up to go, he glared frostily at Topping.

"So that's how you manage to fit in two meetings at the same time—create havoc at the first."

Babu clutched his head. "Ayee, uri mi-ah, what can I do? I must put in order first thing in morning, or booze will not arrive from Calcutta in time for dance." He looked hopefully at Mr. Nightingale, who was on his way out of the door.

"If I were you," said Mr. Nightingale cuttingly, "I'd order the drinks from Delhi—it'll probably be cheaper and better."

"Mr. Topping, sahib, what a mess, what a mess," Babu said when he and Topping were left alone. "I thought you were smart fellow, please everyone."

"But I wanted to," Topping groaned, chewing his knuckles. "But I've never met such a collection of old fogies—they just don't want anything to change, the same thing, year after year."

"Mr. Topping sahib, Apprentice Ball *traditional*," Babu said with dignity as he left.

A few moments later, an Institute bearer appeared at the door. "Sahib, memsahib asking for Papworth sahib. Would not listen when I told her he played cards, had chota peg, gone home."

Mimosa McIntosh pushed through the door. "Bert! Why is everyone lying to me round here? They said you'd gone home."

Topping paled and waved the bearer away. "What on earth are you doing here?" he demanded, feeling sick. His marriage to Mimi had been a ghastly mistake, Lord knows what he'd been thinking about during that leave in Calcutta, he'd been besotted, and she'd lied to him, told him her father was a banker, retired to Scotland, and she'd been visiting friends in Cal. Well, the father had been a banker all right—an Indian one. The mother had been Scottish, rejected by her family, living in poverty since the death of her husband. Topping ignored the lies he had told Mimi, the false name, the important position he held. How was he to know she'd track him down so easily? "I told you not to come, it's very difficult. I told you I would send for you as soon as I could."

"That was months ago. I have barely any money left; Mother's always nagging me. I can't go on, Bert, honest I can't. I must stay with you, you're my husband, after all."

"You can't stay here, Mimi," Topping protested. "You'll

have to go back. It won't be for long, I promise." He opened his wallet and thrust some money at her. "Here—there's a train in about an hour."

"Well, I won't be on it," said Mimosa shortly, taking the money and stuffing it into her bosom. "Promises, promises, that's all I've ever had from you. I'm your wife, Bert, why can't we be together?"

"We can be, just as soon as I get a place."

"I don't understand why you haven't got anywhere yet," she said, sitting on the edge of the committee table and lighting a cigarette. "I had a terrible time tracking you down. First I was directed to an enormous place, swanky as hell. The people were beastly, practically gobbled like turkeys when I told them who I was. A silly bitch with a face like a horse accused me of being 'Daddy's bit of fluff,' called me all kinds of horrible names. Practically accused me of committing bigamy—how was I to know there were two of you with the same name?"

"What else did you tell them?" Topping asked, beginning to sweat.

"Nothing. The old gal stalked in, face as red as a coxcomb, cyanide running in her veins, venom dripping off her tongue. Told me Mr. Papworth was playing cards at the Institute and to sort it out with him." She grinned. "Good thing you were here as well, Bert, or I'd still be roaming around causing no end of trouble for the old goat. Bet the fur's going to be flying when he gets home."

Topping looked at his watch. "I've got a meeting now— you'd better wait for me upstairs." He realised that if in the few minutes he had, he couldn't persuade Mimosa to return to Calcutta, a more immediate concern would be at least to get her out of the way.

There was no one about when he opened the door of the committee room. Quickly he hustled Mimosa out and up the stairs to his flat.

"For goodness' sake, stay put until I come back. I'm booked up for at least an hour. Read a book or something."

Mimosa hooted. "Read a book!" She wandered about,

looking at things. "This is a beautiful flat—why can't I stay here? It's yours, isn't it? Looks like your stuff lying around."

"It's not mine. I'm putting up with a fellow until I find a place. I just can't tell him I want to share his sofa with my wife, he wouldn't go for it at all."

Mimosa was staring in the bedroom. "Well, there's a nice big bed. I'm sure if I asked him, he'd let us have the bed for a few days—it wouldn't hurt him to have the settee—while you have me." She winked.

Topping stared at her in amazement. For the moment he forgot that his room-mate was non-existent. "You'd ask him to move out of his own room?"

"Why not? It would only be for a few days. With me helping to look, we'd soon find somewhere cosy." She came close, put her arms about him. "You haven't even kissed me."

Topping bent his head. Their lips met: his cold, hers passionate, demanding. Slowly his lips opened and merged into hers. He felt a flicker of interest.

"Mmm. I've missed you, Bert. It's been so long."

He let his hands roam over her firm buttocks. He drew her closer to him. She ground her hips into his, started to pull his shirt-tail out of his trousers.

"Bert, Bert!" she panted. With her other hand she drew her skirt up, placed his hand just under the flared legs of her silk drawers.

He turned, hands fumbling buttons, pushed her against the wall, forced a knee between her thighs, pushed them open.

"Bert!" Her hand guided him, he thrust up.

"Oh, Mimi, oh, Mimi."

A little later he sagged against her.

"Bert?"

"Mmm?"

"You didn't use anything, did you."

"Oh my God!"

She smiled. "It doesn't matter, we're together now." She

pulled away. "Just think, right now, your sperm is swimming away inside me, to make our baby." She stroked her stomach, eyes dreamy.

Dazed, Topping staggered downstairs to bump into Joseph Sherman, who was roaming around looking for him.

"Oh, there you are, Topping. No one knew where you'd got to."

"Urgent business," Topping muttered. "Had to talk to someone—"

"We had the musical meeting without you—tried out a few parts and so on. You didn't miss much."

"How was it?"

"They're all very keen—only thing is, the only one with a decent voice is Mrs. Fitter Jones. Boy, can she sing. Like an angel, she is."

"That's fine, fine," Topping said automatically.

"No, it's not," Joseph said, aghast. "She'll have to be the Belle of New York. We'll be a laughing-stock—she must be the ugliest woman in Jamalpur—no, in the entire E.I.R. region."

"Oh God, see what you mean." Topping tried to pull himself together, to get over the horrible shock of what had just occurred upstairs. "Need a drink," he said finally. "Got something in my office. Join me."

In Number 42 Prince's Road, Mrs. Barhill and Jane were looking through magazines. When Jane had informed her mother that Sergeant-Major Barhill had agreed that she could go shopping on the following day for a dance dress, Mrs. Barhill had stared at her speechlessly.

Finally she had said, "He really agreed?"

Jane nodded. "He did—though I think Mary had a lot to do with it. And even when she said to give me plenty of money, he didn't bat an eyelid. Just said I had to be a credit to the Army."

"Amazing," Mrs. Barhill said dryly. "But if he said it,

he must have meant it. However," she paused, considering, "we don't want to kill the golden goose before it's laid the egg. No, my dear, we have to step carefully."

"How do you mean?"

"We can't buy you a store dress, to start with. Your father has no idea, no idea at all, of what they cost, and when he finds out, there'll be hell to pay."

"What about the durzi? Can't he rustle up something decent?"

"Booked up thoroughly. I've already asked him, and that was just for a simple dress for me. You never even entered into the picture." Mrs. Barhill rubbed her neck. "Oh dear, it's so worrying."

"Perhaps we can find something simple in a magazine," Jane suggested. "There's enough time to sew our own—no-one need ever know."

So they sat down, poring over magazines, finally discarding them with a sigh.

"I know!" Jane cried. "What about Wood's box-wallah? He's due next week. We can send him our measurements, tell him what we want. He's very good and very cheap."

Mrs. Barhill brightened. "What a wonderful idea, so clever of you, Jane. We can pay him on the Kathleen Mavorneen system—it may be a year, it may be for ever—but what the heck, everyone does it."

They set about taking measurements, deciding on colours, when the sepoy appeared in the doorway.

"Ray mem," he announced.

Mrs. Ray pushed rudely past and stood staring angrily at Jane. "Well, where is she?" she demanded.

Mrs. Barhill stood up. "Mrs. Ray, after your behaviour in church this morning, I really do not wish to receive you."

"I'm not talking to you, I'm talking to *her*," she said, nodding at Jane.

Mrs. Barhill gasped. "Mrs. Ray—get out!"

"I will when this little hussy here tells me where George O'Leary is, and she needn't tell me she doesn't know because he told me they had an assignation at seven o'clock and"—she consulted her watch with bleary eyes—"it's seven o'clock now."

"You're drunk," declared Mrs. Barhill.

"Not too drunk to claim my man. Where is he?"

"Why don't you try his quarters," said Mrs. Barhill icily. "I'm sure you know the way."

The sepoy hemmed and bowed. "O'Leary sahib tell Sergeant-Major sahib that he go to Tobacco Factory Club. He there now."

Mrs. Ray narrowed her eyes, then tottered out, hailing the gharry that had brought her.

Mrs. Barhill turned to the sepoy. "Peter, is Sergeant O'Leary really at the Tobacco Club?"

Peter grinned. "No, mem—but soon Ray mem will be, and Tobacco Factory Club in Moughyr, long way out of town."

He left the room but returned almost immediately, throwing open the door and announcing, "Jameson sahib."

Mrs. Barhill advanced, her hand outstretched. "How very nice, Jamie, haven't seen you for some time."

James Jameson sat down awkwardly, looking about the room and wriggling. Jane hid a grin. He was noted for his awkwardness, his clumsiness when in the presence of women; the only time he shone was in the field, a gun in his hands.

"Ayah told me you were married," Jane said.

Mrs. Barhill looked astounded. "Don't be so silly, Jane. Of course he's not married." Her expression indicated that James Jameson would never be married, for he would never summon up sufficient courage to ask anyone.

"Oh, yes," he said vaguely, "married, yes, married."

"Married! I don't believe it!"

"Mother not too pleased," he jerked out. "Left m'wife with her, she'll soon talk her round." He looked depressed.

"Well, I never!" Mrs. Barhill exclaimed. She stared at James as if trying to imagine him in bed with a woman, any woman. She suddenly recollected herself. "Why didn't you bring your—hem—wife with you? Like to meet her."

"Fine-looking gel. Met her tiger-hunting."

73

"She shoots?"

"Matter of fact, no. Fact is, she hates it, tells me first thing she's going to do is throw away my guns, ha ha. I was after a couple of man-eaters, stayed with her family for a few days. Father Colonel Armstrong, of the Greys, ever met him?"

Mrs. Barhill nodded. "Top-notch regiment, but I believe I have. Tall, white-haired?"

"That's the chappie. Nice fella, jolly good shot."

"You must have fallen in love very quickly," Jane remarked innocently.

James looked horrified. Hurriedly he changed the subject. "Shot at a couple of tigers. Light bad. Missed one, wounded the other. Trailed 'em a couple of days, but they gave me the slip." James laughed nervously. "Fact is, I picked up the cubs, sweet little fellas. Thought Jane wouldn't mind looking after 'em for a while until I fix it up with a zoo to take 'em."

"I dare say she could," Mrs. Barhill said cautiously, "but she'll have to ask her father."

"Tiger cubs!" Jane exclaimed. "How lovely! Where are they?"


Sonny Edwards was returning home, a dazed man, wondering how the hell to break the news about his sister to Claire, his wife. His pregnant wife.

"Oh God," he groaned. Lunacy in the family, Aunt Matilda a teapot, a cousin a bicycle. Lizzie a bird. Oh Lord, what next? What taint was his unborn child carrying?

What about people? What would they think? Sonny was afraid of public opinion, always hiding behind his wealth, his prowess at sport, his good looks.

How could they hope to hide Lizzie tweeting around the place? Too noisy, and probably start building a nest in the trees next. Lord, what a mess it all was.

He stopped. "Can't go back to face her yet, must think."

He passed Mistri's yard. Mistri was a large Bengali who

74

had an engineering works, as he importantly called it, but which was a general repair shop, full of piles of metal and wooden junk. The pride of Mistri's life were two ramshackle cars, held together by string and wire, which he hired out at exorbitant prices to all the non-whites who didn't know better. Philip was one of his customers; Solomon, when courting, also.

Mistri had his head buried in the bowels of one of his vehicles. Sonny stopped, gazed in, then wandered over and sat down on a packing case. "What's wrong with it, Mistri?" he called out.

Mistri withdrew his head. "Nothing, Sonny sahib, only tuning. Topping sahib say too demn slow, need souping up, so I soup, make it go demn fest car."

"You going anywhere tonight?" enquired Sonny.

"Surely I go, try out on Grand Trunk Road."

"Okay—drop me off at the Tobacco Club, it's on the way."

"Sahib, Tobacco Club four jolly miles far, try out half a mile, maybe."

"I'll pay you," offered Sonny.

"Sahib, how you come back, eh? I not waiting too jolly long, very busy man."

Sonny shrugged. "It doesn't matter. Gharry, I expect, or there'll probably be some Army chappie with a staff car."

An hour later, Sonny was in the club, morosely making his way to the bar. Sitting quite alone on a high bar stool, looking equally dispirited, trying to spear an olive in her gin, was Mrs. Ray.

"Hello, Sonny," she said, brightening visibly. "Come and join me."


An uneasy group was drinking tea in "The Nest." Mrs. Jameson, bloated after a huge dinner of curried minced lamb, had undone the side hooks and eyes of her voluminous black taffeta and was glowering at James's new bride, who was staring back coolly in white linen costume, mannish felt hat, and paper-thin chamois leather gloves that she would not take off.

Urged by her mother to "give us a tune," Jessie had been seated at the oft-raffled piano, Dr. Ray still by her side, giving no indication at all that he ever intended returning home; but now Jessie was wandering about the room wretchedly, waiting for the bombshell to drop. It was imminent; her mother had that look about her.

"More tea, Miss Armstrong?" Mrs. Jameson suggested, waggling the pot.

"No, thank you. I've had five cups."

"Jessie, I'm sure Miss Armstrong would like to see the photo albums."

"I would not care to see the photo albums," Miss Armstrong said calmly, "I abhor photo albums. And pray, do not continue calling me Miss Armstrong. I am now Mrs. Jameson."

Jessie had not expected the first salvo to come from that direction; she shuddered and looked at her mother, who swelled visibly.

"Not to me, you're not," the old woman muttered. "Any woman who grabs the first man who comes along can't be up to much." Her eyes glittered balefully. "If my boy had been at home, you would not have caught him so easily, oh no! I'd have seen through the likes of you right away."

"Mother," Jessie pleaded.

"Shut up, girl. I'm speaking my mind here."

"My husband has already informed me what an old witch you are," Miss Armstrong said, unperturbed. "Why pretend he listens to you? He hasn't listened to you for years."

Jessie suddenly perceived that the play between these two protagonists had been in the making long before James had arrived with his bride. From the moment she had received her son's brief note, Mrs. Jameson had decided to trump Miss Armstrong, to cower her into submission; while Miss Armstrong, in showing her hand so early in the game, was demonstrating her power. Of the three women in the flickering shadows of the kerosene-lit room, only Jessie was embarrassed. The other two were not at all disturbed by this preliminary skirmish; her evil, manipulating old mother and the ruthless Miss Armstrong were laying down the ground-rules for a lifetime of battling.

Looking up, her face laid bare with these illuminating thoughts, Jessie met Dr. Ray's eyes. There was a hint of a conspiratorial wink; he jerked his head towards the door. With a swift glance towards her mother, Jessie slid out of the room. Dr. Ray closed the door gently.

"They're in a different league from you," he said quietly. "They won't even notice you've gone. Shall we sit on the veranda?"

"No, Ayah is smoking her filthy drugs out there." Looking up into the doctor's face, she said, "We won't be disturbed in my room."

He looked searchingly into her eyes. "Are you sure?" he asked with great tenderness.

"Very sure," she replied, suddenly knowing that she was. She had been ready for this for a long time.


Mr. and Mrs. Knowles were still furious. They were still trying, by going over and over Les Topping's comments and behaviour, to discover motives for his insults at the committee meeting.

For the hundredth time, Mrs. Knowles said, "You must have annoyed him. Think back."

"I have thought. There's nothing. Told you, hardly ever see the fella."

"I know!" Mrs. Knowles brightened. "It's Mary."

"Mary?"

"Of course," she said impatiently. "She probably turned him down."

"Didn't know there was anything in the wind between those two. Don't know that I like the idea."

"Oh, don't be so foolish! Mary's got more sense than that—but you know how men are, go overboard for any pretty gel who smiles at them."

"Don't know that he'd take it out on us, though," Mr. Knowles reasoned. "Bit spiteful, what?"

"Oh, womanish men like that Les Topping can be very spiteful. No, mark my words, his pride has been wounded—and somehow it's all our fault." Satisfied that she got to the bottom of the mystery, Mrs. Knowles was content to let the matter rest and prepared to move on to other important items in her agenda, but Mr. Knowles sudenly exclaimed in annoyance and stumped to the door.

"Who can think straight with that confounded cater-wauling. What's going on out there?"

Philip, beautifully turned out in a white drill suit, complete with straw hat and cane, was practising how to tap dance and crooning soulfully, "Darncing with tears in my eyes . . . becawse the garl in my arms sisn't yoooo . . ."

"What's he up to now?" muttered Mr. Knowles.

Mrs. Knowles came up and looked over his shoulder. "Heaven only knows—perhaps he has hopes of being in Les Topping's musical show, fat chance of that."

As they watched, Laksmi appeared, attired in her best silk sari, all her bangles and necklaces on, flowers in her hair.

"Oh my God, so that's the way the land lies, is it?" said Mrs. Knowles. "You'll have to nip it in the bud before there's bloodshed—Charlie's very handy with those meat cleavers."

As soon as he spotted Laksmi, Philip danced more lewdly with hip and eye, substituting his own words for the song. His voice became a subtle wooing, an enticing throb. Laksmi smiled and glanced down modestly.

Song over, Philip pranced up to Laksmi. "We go now, I got Mistri's car, we go big bang car ride, jolly good time we be having."

"Stop them," Mrs. Knowles urged, giving her husband a push.

Mr. Knowles advanced into the compound. "Philip," he shouted. "Here at once."

Philip whirled about, as if shot, and shuffled shame-facedly towards Mr. Knowles. "Only singing, sahib, only singing."

"What's this about car ride with Charlie's woman? I forbid it, d'you hear?"

"Only taking Laksmi to visit her mother, mother very sick, sahib. Pheelip very good driver, very carefully I'm going."

"You're not going anywhere with Laksmi, carefully or not. I'm not having trouble between you and Charlie."

"But, sahib, Charlie playing cards, he not find out."

As he spoke, Charlie appeared as if on cue and grabbed his wife by the arm. "What goin' on here, eh? What you wearing wedding clothes, for, eh? All togged up mighty fine—what for, eh?"

Laksmi drooped like a spent flower. She salaamed before her husband. "I dress for you; for you, I dress fine clothes. Laksmi think you play cards all time, you maybe tired of wife."

"I think you tell husband lies. It's a beating I am giving you immediately, plenty big beating," Charlie yelled, shaking Laksmi, dragging her off back to their quarters.

"Ayee, ayee," Philip moaned, clutching his head. "Mighty fine night, all gone up creek."

"You'll be up the creek if Charlie comes at you with his meat cleavers," said Mr. Knowles. "Now take off those silly clothes, you are not a sahib, and stay with the men until you have your own woman."

Philip looked sulky. "Father Millet, he give me clothes, you ask him. Uri mi-ah, uri mi-ah," he added as screams came from the servants' quarters. "Tell Charlie he no good shaitan, he stop beating Laksmi," he begged. "Laksmi, all black and blue she will be for sure."

"If she is, it'll be your fault," Mr. Knowles said, exasperated. "Perhaps she'll stop playing around and be a good wife—she's only been married a week, she deserves a good beating. Now take that car back to Mistri, go on, be off with you."

Philip brightened. "Ayee, I go jolly good car ride, mighty fine bang-bang. Find other woman."

Cheerfully he minced off, twirling the cane. Sighing, Mr. and Mrs. Knowles looked at each other.

"It's been a long day," said Mr. Knowles. "I'm going fishing in the reservoir."

# THE
# SECOND
# SUNDAY

Dawn stole across the Seven Sisters, illuminating the black Queen Victoria in glory. Under her lofty chin, a tiger roared. Mrs. Jameson's cows and goats moved about uneasily in their stalls before the goats decided the danger was real and set up a clamour.

Jessie stirred in her sleep. Surely it was too early to milk? Then she remembered and smiled, stretching out a hand to stroke her beloved. Her hand encountered nothing. Dr. Ray had gone; the half of the bed that had been his for a week was empty.

Panic-stricken, Jessie sat up and looked about her wildly. "Jeremy?" She saw him standing by the window, a dark shadow against the pale grey dawn. "Oh, Jeremy, I thought you'd—"

She broke off, feeling foolish, and slid out of bed. He held one arm out for her, and she snuggled close to his side. The familiar feeling grew in sweetness; honey ran through her veins.

"You know I'm not going to leave you," he said, stroking her breasts. "You know that, don't you?"

"I'm not used to you yet," she murmured. "It doesn't seem real, you being here. It's only been a week."

"A week. Has it been as long as that? I'll have to go home—though I doubt she's even missed me."

"Oh, no! I can't bear it." She clung to him, burying her face in his chest.

"I'll have to go," he said, stroking her river of hair, silvered in the misty light. "I can't hide away here for ever—got to sort out my life, my work, a divorce—"

Her face shone, eyes lifted up to his. "A divorce?"

"We'll have to go to England, I dare say. Start again. You know what it's like, being divorced out here."

"England!" she said. The word was an exultation.

"Listen," he said, gazing out of the window. "Did you hear that?"

"The goats, you mean? For some reason they think it's milking time."

"No, not the goats. Sounded like a tiger to me."

"A tiger!" She was not frightened, but still, in a womanly way, she clung close.

"Don't worry—probably up in the hills. The last time a tiger was seen on the Maidan was in 1800," he said gruffly, protectively.

"Perhaps it was the soldiers out on the rifle range," Jessie suggested, feeling the honey in her veins richen and quicken. "Come to bed," she whispered. Farmyard images throbbed through her mind: glistening red, thrusting, spurting.

"Oh God," she groaned. "Quickly, I can't wait."


In the suite of rooms above the library at the Institute, Vivien Papworth fumbled her hand from under the mosquito netting to reach for the clock. She knocked over a glass half-filled with a moribund mixture of port and lemonade that Topping had promised her would absolutely ensure that she would wake without a hangover, and shuddered as the sticky liquid ran down her arm.

"Oh God, how yucky." Wiping her arm on the bottom sheet, she hauled the top sheet off Topping's recumbent body and draped it around herself. "Les, wake up—I've got to get home before the servants start buzzing around." She prodded him with her foot. "Wake up."

"Can't," groaned Topping. "Beastly headache." But somehow he managed first to sit upright, then to crawl out of bed. Pale and trembling, he stood clutching the post at the foot of the bed. "Drank too much," he mumbled. "Going to throw up."

"Get me some water," Vivien commanded. "I need to clean up."

Wincing with distaste, Topping shuffled to the simple, tiled room that sufficed as a bathroom. Some water still remained in the kettle the old mali had provided for shaving. It was cold, but would have to do.

"Darling," Vivien drawled behind him, "how utterly primitive. You don't really expect me to sponge myself down with a kettle of water, do you?"

"It's all I have—we don't exactly run to Carlton amenities here," Topping muttered. He nodded towards the windows. "Unless you fancy going swimming, plenty of water out there, wash all your sins away." Oh my God, had he really said that?

"Don't be sulky, darling," Vivien replied, taking the kettle. "If it's all you've got, it will have to do—but really, darling, I would have thought you'd at least have arranged a shower up here if you intend to go in for this sort of thing." She splashed some water in a bowl and surveyed Topping over her shoulder. "Really, darling, cover yourself up. You look positively anaemic. I like my men hairy, like gorillas."

Topping stared at her, dazed. All his aspirations as a social climber had led him to suppose that upper-crust girls like Vivien Papworth had class, elegance, but she was nothing but a slut, worse than Mimi. But he had to stop thinking about Mimi.

"You didn't object last night," he said, holding a towel up like a shield.

"Darling, I never complain in bed, and it was dark," Vivien said, sponging herself down.

"I thought you loved me. You said—"

"Love!" She trilled with laughter. "No, darling, just a bit of fun."

"I thought we were going to get married," he said, seeing all his dreams fade away. He'd spent weeks baiting his hook, angling, and now this!

"Now, now, don't be so plebeian. With all my worldly goods I thee endow, including the kettle. How dreadfully dreary, too romantic by half. Anyway, Daddy would die, he'd simply die with shock, poor dear."

"What would Daddy say if he knew about us?" Topping sneered as Vivien padded around the bedroom collecting her clothes.

She struggled into her bra. "Oh dear, don't be so boring, darling. Daddy would probably turn purple and have you thrown out on your arse if you were caddish enough to tell him about us. Apart from that, I don't suppose he'd care very much." She sauntered to the door and blew him a kiss. "Do something about a shower if you want us to do this again—I feel positively filthy. This place is too second-rate by half."

Les Topping sank onto his bed, head in his hands. The bitch, the little bitch. Her mocking words echoed through his head. Oh God, what a mess. And he thought he'd got her eating out of his hand, thought his charm and polish had captivated her. To her it was just a game. He groaned. What a fool—a kingdom lost over a kettle.

But in his heart he knew it was more than that. It was the bloody invisible line between her class and his class. Oh God, it was too bloody unfair. "Bloody unfair," he shouted. She could be as uncouth and as common as a street slut, but still, she was to the manner born and all that. And he, for all his airs and cultivated graces, would always, always be recognised for what he was. An upstart.

At "Cader Idris," Claire lay silently in a narrow bed and stared through the fine mesh of the mosquito netting at the ceiling.

The fan moved slowly, stirred only by the breeze from the open window. This had been her childhood bed, and now she was back in it, carrying her own child in her womb.

Her child. Hers and Joseph's.

"You've got to get rid of it," Sonny had told her. "It'll probably turn out to be crackers—like everyone else in our family."

"Rid of it?" she had mumbled foolishly.

"Edna says she knows someone who'll fix it up," he jerked out. "Says that's why she's never had a kid—knew about it all along, Aunt Edna and great-grandfather who thought he was Nelson one week and Saint Peter the next. Then there turns out to be a cousin who was a bicycle. Said she never knew about him, though."

Bewildered, Claire stared at him. "What on earth are you talking about?" she asked. "Have you taken leave of your senses?"

Her choice of words was unfortunate. Bursting into tears, Sonny had poured it all out, about Aunt Edna, the skeletons of lunacy in the family closet—and now Lizzie. He concluded by confessing that he had spent the night with Mrs. Ray in the grounds of the Rajah's Palace on the Moughyr Road.

"Worthless, worthless," he had sobbed.

Very indignant about Mrs. Ray, Claire had been, but it made her feel better about herself and Joseph.

Somewhere in the mess, in the noisy sobbing, the snot running down the lip, the clutching at her knees as he grovelled on the floor, Sonny had repeated that she was to get rid of the baby.

"No," she said very clearly. And with quiet dignity, she had packed a bag and removed herself to her mother's house.

"Joseph's child?" Mrs. Darsi Jones repeated when the whole sorry tale had been told her. "You can't be telling anyone, can you now?"

"Why not?" Claire asked.

"Because of the money, girl, use your loaf," Mrs. Darsi Jones said practically. "Going to inherit millions, Sonny is.

It's cutting your nose off to spite your face, you are, if you tell him the nipper's not his."

Claire was astounded. "But he wants me to have an abortion. I tell you, he doesn't want the baby. His own child—" She remembered and coloured. "Well, the child he thinks is his. He doesn't want it. Thinks it's going to be born loopy-lou."

"Well, you know it's not, so that's all that counts, isn't it?" said Mrs. Darsi Jones. "Seems to me, it's all worked out for the best."

Claire started to giggle hysterically. "Ma, you're priceless. So you think I should stay with Sonny and let him think the child is his—just let him worry for the rest of his life, wondering when it's going to go round the bend?"

"No reason why it should, even if it were his," said Mrs. Darsi Jones. "I mean to say, girl, just because there's lunacy in the family doesn't mean that everyone has to go mad, now does it? Think of the shame, girl, if Sonny divorces you. Think how sorry you'll be when you're old and in the workhouse."

"Oh, Ma!" Claire exclaimed. "Why, you're an old hypocrite."

"No, it's sensible I am. Mark my words, tell Sonny the truth and you'll live to regret it."

"But what about him and Mrs. Ray?" Claire said petulantly. "He spent the night rolling about the Maharajah's lawns with that tramp."

"Men are like that, you have to make allowances," said Mrs. Darsi Jones placidly.

So Claire had spent a week holed up in her mother's house, refusing to talk to Sonny, refusing to answer Edna's notes, refusing in fact to even think about any of it. During the day she read, played the piano, sewed, lazed in the garden, acquiring a lovely honey-coloured illegal tan—a tan that seemed to offend her mother far more than the morals involved in her delicate situation.

"It's chee-chee you're wanting to be now, is it?" Mrs. Darsi Jones cried in horror. "What will everyone be saying when my daughter turns up at the Apprentices' Ball as black as a wog? It's ashamed I'll be. Get inside, girl, and cover yourself up."

"Oh, Mother," Claire sighed, stuffing a slice of mango in her mouth. "The sun's good for you. Nectar of the gods."

But during the quiet nights, she lay in her narrow bed and pined for Joseph. Not once had he made an effort to approach her. A secret doubt gnawed at her. Was her mother right? Was Joseph hanging on to loud, vulgar Edna for her share of the family fortune?

If she didn't see him before, she resolved to confront him at the Apprentices' Ball. Beautiful she would look that night. Her gown, a dream of sea-green chiffon with violet ribbons the colour of her lustrous eyes, hung in the closet wrapped in a sheet.

Beautiful she would look, and Joseph would die of love for her.


At Mrs. Ray's, Sonny yawned luxuriously and stretched out a languid hand for the Bloody Mary Mrs. Ray had prepared for him personally. His hair was tousled and boyish. "This is the life," he sighed. "Beats an early morning cuppa."

"I'll say," said Mrs. Ray, perching on the edge of the big double bed and sipping her own gin and Rose's lime juice. He looked vulnerable, like a schoolboy who had strayed; she felt moved to make a momentous comment. "Tell you what, Sonny—you're my kind of man. Know how to have fun, none of this moaning and whining about drinking too much, or having to get home to the wife."

"Claire's left me," Sonny said. "Gone home to mother."

"Best place for her," said Mrs. Ray. "What you want, Sonny, is a real woman."

"And what you want," said Sonny, "is a real man."

Pleased with their pronouncements, they smiled at each other, and Mrs. Ray stroked Sonny's foot.

"I say," he said after several minutes of pure ecstasy, "where's Jeremy?"

"Oh him," said Mrs. Ray casually. "I don't know. Haven't seen him for days. Come on—move over, make room for me."

Mr. Knowles was fishing. He had arrived at the reservoir late the previous night, Saturday, and contentedly had sat in the velvet darkness, dozing, dreaming, soaking in the quiet beauty of the hills and the glorious stars.

Somewhere towards dawn, Mistri had arrived; both were great rivals for the J.M.P. fishing cup.

"Got a new bait, Mistri," said Mr. Knowles. "Rice beer balls—care to try some?"

"No, sa'b," said Mistri. "I'll stick to atta laced with fine mince."

"You're never touching meat!" exclaimed Mr. Knowles. "Won't you lose caste? Thought meat was untouchable."

"Surely," said Mistri. "This is goat, got very good, very strong stink. Goat used in much sacrifice, the gods will be much pleased, drive all the fish to hook."

Mr. Knowles tried some on his fingers. "Phew, they'll probably faint with shock when this hits the water. Hope it's not as strong as it smells—you'll poison half the town. We'll be getting complaints; they'll ban us from fishing, accuse us of peeing in the water, or something."

They settled down on their meechans, their torches lighting up the floats. For a spell they fished in silence, until Mr. Knowles noted a beam of light on the opposite bank. "Mistri," he called. "We seem to have company."

"I am noticing, sa'b. Many nights we have company. Some very noisesome. Last week there was much splashings, driving fishes away."

"Amateurs," said Knowles. "Why don't they use the reservoir in the daytime? That chappie isn't going to have much luck, anyway—picked the part with most weeds."

"He will be making big loss of line and hook," agreed Mistri. "Maybe losing rod also. Better he stay there than disturb us with much splashings about."

They lapsed into silence. There was a slight wind which gently ruffled the surface of the water, causing the fishing lines to ripple and the floats to bob. The reservoir was quite beautiful at night. It was framed in a background of dark hills, mysterious against the purple sky, while closer at hand was a symmetrical, wooded hill, crowned with a castle-like structure, which was, in fact, the pumping station. A favorite walk for moony lovers was the curving avenue of sweet-scented cork trees leading to the mock castle. The only sounds were echoes from the Railway Station (which never slept) and the tom-tom beaters.

The moon slid from behind piled clouds, silvering the rippling waves, edging the sweet corks with light. Mr. Knowles felt happiest when fishing at night. The peace of his surroundings and its softened beauty laid quiet fingers on his mind and soothed away all the annoyances and trivialities of the day. Even if he missed going to bed, he felt as rested as if he had slept a full eight hours.

Mistri was the first to break the long silence as his rod flashed up. "I am making a big catch," he called out. His rod bowed in an arc. "Bloody son of shaitan," he swore heartily, teeth gleaming, "he is a veritable monster, trying to pull Mistri in. Ho ho, Mistri not accepting invitation, no bloody fear." He reeled in some line. "Make jump! Make jump!" he cried to the fish. "Jump! Be showing us what magnificent fish you are!"

"Ho, Mali!" shouted Mr. Knowles to his sleeping servant. "Help Mistri babu, quick, quick!"

The mali uncurled himself, protesting. It was a mystery to him why his master spent so many hours of the night staring at an expanse of water, when he could be cheating on his wife instead.

"Mali, mali!" Mr. Knowles shouted again. To Mistri, he said, "Watch it, you'll lose it."

"I am watching. Deadweight it is, and fighting at bottom of water. Cunning this one is, no splashings, no running to tire and waste its strength, oh, mighty fine, cunning fish." He reeled in some more line.

The yawning mali waded into the water as if feeling his way into a quicksand, convinced that he was about to sink up to his neck in the inky water, and making little attempt to catch the fish.

Mr. Knowles noticed his own float jerk down and yanked his rod up. The slender bamboo tip arched into the water. "I've got one too, Mistri," he shouted. He reeled in some line. "Must be a relation," he joked. "It's not splashing, either."

With little help from the mali, both fishermen expectantly reeled in their lines and landed their catches. Silently, they stared at two cloth-covered bundles, dripping with weeds and slime.

"Not fish, I'm thinking, sahib," said Mistri. "Treasure, maybe. Gold and silver from the Rajah's palace, maybe."

"Well, let's open them and have a look," said Mr. Knowles, bending down and slashing the string on one bundle with his fishing knife.

"Krishna!" gasped Mistri, dropping his torch.

Mr. Knowles stared silently at a swollen head, as turgid as the belly of a rotting fish. Only the scarlet lips, obscene against the leprous skin, and the drowned fronds of yellow-green hair proclaimed that once this had been a woman. Water-snails sucked greedily at her tongue.

"Doesn't look as if the gods took kindly to your sacrifice of the goat," Mr. Knowles finally joked, clutching at words inanely. "Can't say I want to look in the other parcel."

"Uri-bab, uri-bab," Mistri moaned, "I am thinking there is some funny business here, very funny business, oh, yes, sa'b, no good for Mistri's reputation. Me, I think I go home now."

"Better hang about," Mr. Knowles said. "The police might not like it if you clear off—you know what the police are like."

"Oh, my goodness, the police. I am not very happy, most distressed by all these happenings," Mistri moaned, wiping his brow. He sat down on the bank and dolefully stared at the unwrapped parcel. "One head or two heads?" he asked.

"I don't know, and I intend to leave it up to the police to find out," said Mr. Knowles grimly. "Mali," he directed, "you better go to police lines and call Superintendent Higgins sahib. We will wait here."

"I am thinking I am very ill," Mistri said as the mali hurried off. "I am thinking I am hearing roarings in my head."

"You know, I think you're right," said Mr. Knowles, staring at the hills. "Odd noises, almost sound like tigers."

"If not tigers, some large cat creatures making big noises."

"Tigers," said Mr. Knowles with conviction, "were last seen on the Maidan in 1800. That's a long time ago. Those graves in the middle of the Maidan are of a tiger and the man it killed." He shook his head. "No, it can't be tigers. We're just feeling edgy. These parcels have spooked us."

"Incredibly spooky night, sa'b," said Mistri. "There is much jolly spookiness all around us; it is not good to stay here. I'm thinking we are better at home, nice cup of cha."

"That reminds me." Mr. Knowles dug in his fishing bag. "Can't offer you tea, but—" He produced a bottle of Dimple Haigh. "Have some."

Mistri looked shocked. "Sa'b, I do not drink!" But he took the bottle, uncorked the top, and with practised ease, poured some straight down his throat.

From the hills, the tigers roared again.


When the dawn broke, the Reverend Morgan Morgan could be seen on his knees in the vicarage garden, where he had spent the entire night. Within, on the dining-room table, like a houri, tempting, beckoning, was a full bottle of Booth's and a clean glass.

But Morgan Morgan knew that the only way he would be able to do his duty to God that morning, as the Reverend

Cuthbert Pritchard's temporary replacement, was to lock himself out of the house and do battle with the devils within him in his own private Gethsemane.

Many times in the night he had contemplated breaking in, and had even picked up a stout cudgel to aid him; but the servants had been given their orders, and when they saw him make some furtive moves, banged on the windows, beat on tom-toms, and shouted most excitedly.

"Thank you, thank you, brothers," Morgan Morgan groaned, sinking to his knees again. Stiff they were, and cold he was; but the houri mocked in vain.

By dawn he had a raging thirst upon him and felt he could not go on much longer. With an effort, he raised his eyes to the black hills and started to pray.

"I lift up my eyes to the hills... and you are there, oh, Avril, my Avril..."

Somehow improvisation crept in, and Avril shimmered up there on the slopes, wraithlike, virginal.

"Oh my dove, thou art in the clefts of the rock.... Silent are the hills... silent is the dawn... silent is the sound of your voice.... Avril, my Avril..."

Alternately weeping and praying, Morgan Morgan rocked himself into a kind of hypnotic trance, the garbled words pouring out; sometimes in English, sometimes in Welsh, like a song they flowed, rich and strong in cadence.

The mali, passing on his way to the police station, was most impressed. "A truly holy man," he muttered, salaaming vigorously before hurrying on his way.

M̲rs. Knowles and Mary were having breakfast when Solomon presented his mistress with a note.

Mrs. Knowles opened it. "Oh Lord," she sighed, "it's from Miss Toogood, reminding me that I'd promised to ride round the Maidan with her this morning before church. But I don't have time—I simply don't have the time."

"Well, tell her so," Mary replied, spooning fresh cream over some green figs.

"I can't, I can't. I've cancelled twice already—they'll think I'm so rude."

Solomon salaamed quietly. "Missie sahib jolly good bicyclist," he murmured. "Make wheels go round most fast. Zenana mem will be getting very fine exercise, most exhausted she will be, perhaps not want to go again."

"Solomon, you're a genius!" Mrs. Knowles exclaimed. "Why didn't I think of that?"

"Probably because you knew I'd refuse," Mary replied. "Those old biddies get on my nerves—what on earth shall I talk about?"

"Nothing—you'll be too busy saving your breath for pedalling," Mrs. Knowles said. "Go on, girl, earn your keep for a change."

"I can't. I've promised to sweet-talk Sergeant-Major Barhill into letting Jane go for a walk with me after church this morning."

Mrs. Knowles paused in drinking a cup of tea and gazed consideringly at her daughter. "What are you up to now?" she demanded.

"Nothing," Mary replied innocently. "Just going for a walk, up to the pumping station. It's a lovely morning."

"Well, you can sweet-talk the Sergeant-Major into letting Jane go with you round the Maidan with Miss Toogood *before* church, and the pumping station *after*," Mrs. Knowles said firmly. "And talking about the pumping station, your father's been fishing a long time."

"Probably fallen asleep," Mary said. "You know he and his cronies drink their heads off like the proverbial fish they're trying to catch, and pass out."

"Your father," said Mrs. Knowles with dignity, "fishes. He brings home some excellent catches. I dare say he's found himself a good spot and has forgotten the time."

Sergeant-Major Barhill was involved with some disciplinary matters in the Regiment.

"Jolly good," said Mary chirpily. "He can't possibly object to you riding around with one of the vestal virgins, now can he?"

Jane looked doubtful "You'd think not," she agreed. "But after a rush of magnanimity last week—thanks to you—his sphincter tightened up again, and he's been his usual rotten self ever since."

"He hasn't changed his mind about letting you go to the dance, has he?"

"No." Jane grinned faintly. "He promised, remember? But he'll do his damndest to see I have a beastly time; probably make me sit with the dowagers all evening." She looked hopefully at her mother. "Can I go with Mary?"

"I don't see why not," Mrs. Barhill replied. "Your father will not return until lunchtime. If he comes back earlier, I'll tell him Miss Blenkinsop requested your presence—that'll shut him up. In awe of Miss Blenkinsop, he is. Told me once she reminded him of his junior-school headmistress."

"Good grief, anyone would think we were going into the red-light district in Calcutta instead of round the park less than quarter of a mile away," Jane burst out as they pedalled away. "I wish someone would shoot the old bugger—he's not normal. Nice funeral, and then la dolce vita in J.M.P."

"Funny thing is he's not religious," Mary said, giggling. "It's usually the religious maniacs who see sin and sex lurking around every corner. Their minds are so dirty they need sweeping out."

"I wonder if Miss Toogood can ride?" Jane said as the gates of the Zenana Mission came into sight.

"Pretty fancy place," said Mary as they pedalled up the long drive between an avenue of handsome trees. "Goodness, I never knew they had a swimming pool!"

"Look as if they live like millionaires," Jane agreed, dismounting before the rambling white stone building covered with luscious trailing vines and roses.

The door was answered by a young Indian girl in a long calico sack with a high neck and long sleeves. Her hair was dragged back and hidden in a veil. She salaamed and bid them wait.

"Goodness, why do the servants here have to dress like that?" Mary whispered. "She'd be so much more comfortable in a sari."

"Too heathenish," pronounced Jane as Miss Blenkinsop and Miss Harris arrived.

"Sorry, Mother can't make it," Mary announced. "I've come instead."

Miss Blenkinsop frowned. "You're too young—how can I allow Miss Toogood to be chaperoned by a person younger than herself?"

"There's two of us," Mary countered gravely. "Surely that will do?"

"The Maidan is not safe; far too many frivolous and dangerous men roaming around there. I'm surprised your mothers have agreed to this," said Miss Blenkinsop.

"My father's fishing at the reservoir," Mary improvised. "He's going to keep an eye out for us."

"Well—"

"So kind," chirped Miss Harris, hobbling forward. "Miss Toogood won't be a moment; Miss Blenkinsop suggested she change her clothes."

Goodness, just like my father and the hat, thought Jane, amazed. Too saucy, too saucy.

"I can't say I approve of your dress," Miss Blenkinsop said sourly, looking from Mary to Jane. "They are not at all suitable, those frocks. What happens when the wind blows? It is not good to show so much leg. Puts ideas into men's minds, and they certainly don't need much encouragement."

Mary struggled to keep a straight face as Miss Toogood emerged in a pair of long navy-blue bloomers and a high-necked coolie-style coat. No flesh showed and no female shape.

"Remember, Miss Toogood, you are bicycling for your health and not for your pleasure," Miss Blenkinsop admonished.

Miss Toogood bobbed her head meekly, smiled anxiously at Mary and Jane, and led the way out of the house. Her ancient bicycle was waiting, wheeled in place by the girl in the calico sack.

"Miss Blenkinsop suggested fifty circuits of the Maidan," said Miss Toogood.

"Hum," Mary responded, biting back a strong retort, thinking she would have a few words to say to her mother if she survived this experience. Fifty circuits, indeed—why that was over a hundred miles. Miss Blenkinsop was crazier than she thought.

They emerged from the dense screen of trees hiding the Mission from public view and swung into Consort Road, red dust swirling in their wake.

"Awful, aren't they?" puffed Miss Toogood.

"Who?" asked Mary.

"Not who, the clothes," said Miss Toogood, depressed. "But dear Miss Blenkinsop, she means well."

"She may mean well," Mary said sarcastically, "but she doesn't think well. People like her have such dirty minds, talk about soot-fall! All they seem to think of is sex; anyone would think they were perverted or very frustrated."

"There is a lot of sin about," Miss Toogood said softly. "You need a shield against it."

"Hum," said Mary again, not convinced.

"She's a very good woman," Miss Toogood insisted, pedalling hard to keep up with Mary, while Jane trailed in their wake. "And a very sick one. Spent most of her life in a leper mission in Bhagalpur, and now she's a leper, too."

"Holy cow!" Mary squealed, nearly falling off her bicycle. "She's got a nerve going about in public. And what about you?"

"There is no danger," Miss Toogood said calmly. "I mean that one just has to be careful, that's all. When it shows in her face, as it will, she has arranged to go to a leper colony. She's a real saint, you know."

Struck speechless, Mary pedalled an entire circuit without opening her mouth. She could see the reservoir as they swung round a curve, and there seemed to be a flurry of activity going on up there. "Looks as if they're getting steam up for the J.M.P. cup," she remarked.

"Indeed, I love fishing," Miss Toogood said eagerly. "Perhaps Miss Blenkinsop would allow me to do some if you will accompany me."

"Best fishing's at night," said Mary. "Even my parents would draw the line at that."

They turned the corner past the vicarage and a sudden gust of wind tweaked at Miss Toogood's veil as it streamed behind her and carried it away. Swirling and dipping like a plume of smoke, it sailed across the Maidan. Jane set off in pursuit, bumping over the grass. A horseman galloped towards her, hooves thundering, tail tossing. He saw the veil, turned his horse, and swooped down upon the scrap of grey.

Leaping lightly from the saddle, he bowed. "Your scarf, ma'am."

Jane stared into the bluest, most dazzling, most earth-shattering eyes in the entire world. Fair-haired, white teeth; tall, bold, broad-shouldered. A pirate, an outlaw, a ravisher of women, a prince!

"Thank you," she said numbly, making no move to take the veil.

"Mother of God," he burst out, "from the time I first saw you I've not been able to get you out of my mind."

Jane stared at him, eyes open wide in query.

"It can't be, I thought, a little governess, a piano teacher. Don't get involved, you don't need complications."

"But where—?"

"At the Maharajah's palace—you were teaching the daughters. You didn't see me. But who would be dreaming I would be finding my lost queen in this godforsaken land?" He reached for Jane's hand and kissed it. "MacNamara, rightful king of Ireland," he declared, laughing with pleasure at the serendipitous moment. Dazed, Jane stared at him, her hazel eyes wide with shock. "It doesn't happen like this," she said, half to herself. "It just doesn't."

99

\* \* \*

Sonny had gone off to play tennis, although Mrs. Ray seriously doubted that he would be able to focus on the ball, let alone hit it. However, she kissed him good-bye and now, thoroughly bored, was roaming about her bungalow, bottle of gin in one hand, glass in the other. Moodily, she stared out of a window.

What to do, what to do? Already her exhausting night with Sonny was fading; she was ready for more fun.

"George O'Leary!" she said, as if making a sudden discovery. Time she tracked him down; after a week he would be ripe for the plucking.

She made up carefully: powder, rouge, slash of scarlet across mouth, green shadow, spit on mascara, and cake lashes. Flame-coloured sun-dress, high-heeled sandals, wide-brimmed straw hat, scarlet ribbons. Squirt, squirt, Nuit de Paris. Very nice. Summoning a gharry, she set off for the Regimental lines.

"George, George!" Mrs. Ray banged on Sergeant O'Leary's door.

A sepoy, squatting on the ground under a banyan tree, spat out a stream of pan, staining the ground bright red. "Sergeant sahib gone out, room very empty."

Mrs. Ray ignored him. "George!" She banged harder. "I know you're in there."

"Sahib gone out, sahib in office with Sergeant-Major sahib."

"Shut up, go to hell," snarled Mrs. Ray.

"I go," agreed the sepoy. "But Sergeant Sahib still not in."

Mrs. Ray stared at him. He stared back, shifting the pan in his mouth and chewing, rocking on his haunches.

"Blast," she muttered. Tottering on her heels since she had dismissed the gharry, she stormed to the Regimental offices. Pushing the sentry aside she flung the door open, glaring at the figure kneeling on the floor, sorting through files.

"If you think you can ignore me for a week and get away with it—" she started, stopping short as Sergeant-Major Barhill rose and glared at her.

"Madam, what is the meaning of this intrusion?" he asked icily.

"But this is Sergeant O'Leary's office," she said, ignoring his tone. "Where is he?"

"Madam, I don't know, and I don't care," said the Sergeant-Major. "Sentry!" he called out. "Escort this female from Army property."

The sentry appeared, bayonet at the ready, and tripped on the door-sill.

Mrs. Ray screamed as the point pierced her posterior. "You bastard, you've stabbed me."

The sentry stood to attention, his eyes showing white under his turban. "Sa'b, sa'b," was all he managed to utter.

Mrs. Ray clapped a hand to her rump, then started screaming horribly as she saw blood. "You won't get away with this, inciting a wog to attack a white woman. I'll have your hide for this."

"Madam," said Sergeant-Major Barhill in an awful voice, "this is a Regimental Office, not a bazaar. I'll have you arrested for trespass. Now, do you wish to accompany the corporal to the M.O., or do you wish to have him summon a gharry?"

"I'm not having your filthy doctors messing about with my arse," Mrs. Ray snarled.

"Why not—everyone else has," the Sergeant-Major said, unperturbed.

Mrs. Ray glared venomously at him. "Get me a gharry, and get it here fast before I bleed to death," she said. "And while you're about it, get me a bloody drink. A large gin."

Mr. Nightingale decided it was time he called on Les Topping to see what was happening with arrangements for the Apprentices' Ball. When all was said and done, it couldn't fizzle out simply because the committee didn't see eye to eye.

The bearer knocked on Topping's door. "Sahib, sahib."

Topping had collapsed back in bed after Vivien Papworth's crushing exit. Now he sat up, groaning. "What d'you want?" he shouted.

"Nightingale sahib."

"Oh God," Topping muttered. "Okay, tell the sahib to give me five minutes, stomach out of order. I'll be right down. Put him in my office and give him a drink, or some tea or something."

Topping shaved hurriedly in the remains of Vivien's dirty water, cutting himself and dabbing bits of hard bog-roll all over his face. He dragged on his clothes and ran downstairs to his office.

"Morning, sir," he said, holding out his hand.

Nightingale ignored the hand. "What on earth have you done to your face?" he asked. "You look diseased."

"Oh, Christ." Topping ran to a mirror and started peeling off the paper; some of the cuts opened and dripped blood onto his white collar. "Cut myself shaving," he mumbled. "Feel beastly this morning, stomach out of order."

"Well, what have you done about the ball?" Nightingale began without preamble. "Mr. Grundy and I have waited a week for some indication of how you propose to arrange it, and not a word. We now have only five days."

Topping smiled brightly, not realising how ghastly he looked. "I haven't exactly wasted my time. The decorations and the layouts of the rooms have been taken care of. That only leaves the catering." He coughed. "I was wrong," he admitted nobly. "Actually, misinformed." He coughed again discreetly. "Knowles is the best man, I can see that now."

"Misinformed by whom?" demanded Nightingale. "We certainly did not misinform you."

"Oh! No, not you, sir," said Topping, putting on his naïve little boy act, which that morning was at odds with his haggard condition. "Miss Papworth led me astray, sir."

Well, it wasn't exactly a lie, Topping thought maliciously.

"Miss Papworth?" Nightingale said, startled. "Miss Vivien Papworth?"

"Yes, sir. Said her father found the previous balls too—" He searched for a telling phrase. "Too second-rate and plebeian. Boring."

"Hum," muttered Nightingale, taken aback. "Boring, eh?"

"Yes, sir, that's what she said." Topping waited.

"Hum." Nightingale cleared his throat. "Did she give any indication of what her father expected?" he finally asked.

"No, sir. Just said he thought it should be more exciting. 'Seductive,' actually, was the word she used."

"Seductive?" Nightingale repeated uneasily. "Her father said that?"

"No," Topping said carefully, "she said that. But she did imply it was the kind of thing he wanted. More fun. A theme."

"Oh, I see. A theme!" Nightingale nodded. "What kind of theme?"

"Well, sir, I realise that her suggestions are quite out of the question—"

"Well—?"

"She wants, well, she wants a kind of Arabian Nights theme, with everyone practically naked. As a matter of fact," he paused modestly, "she has just left. I told her, of course, that the Institute couldn't go in for that kind of thing."

"No, of course not." Nightingale stared at the carpet. "But Mr. Papworth wants something along those lines? Not the extreme lines that Miss Papworth was suggesting, of course." He paced the room. "We could make the decorations Eastern—couldn't we?"

Topping nodded, smirking inside. "And the band—I don't think they'd object to Eastern outfits, but beyond that, it's definitely not on. The ladies just wouldn't go for it, naked bellies and so on."

"Good Lord," said Nightingale, "I should think not."

"And about Mr. Knowles, sir, I was only trying to do what Mr. Papworth wanted. Bit of razzle-dazzle and all that."

"Yes, yes," said Mr. Nightingale, "you should have told us where it all came from. This puts quite a different complexion on the whole affair. Don't worry about it, m'boy— we'll back you up." He shook Topping by the hand. "Loyalty, that's a good quality in a man. Jolly good show."

Topping sank into his chair when Nightingale had left and tossed a large amount of Scotch down his throat.

At the reservoir, Superintendent Higgins and a bevy of his underlings were buzzing about, taking measurements, taking statements, taking notes, fishing more dripping bundles out of the water. Chasing off flies.

With the heat of the sun, hordes of flies had descended upon the reeking bundles—there were now four—and Mr. Knowles's Dimple Haigh had been seconded to calm several squeamish stomachs.

Amid eager cries a water-logged handbag was fished out by its strap. Superintendent Higgins cautiously emptied its gummy contents onto his outspread handkerchief. He found a soggy photograph and with narrowed eyes compared it with the swollen fish-head shrouded in canvas at his feet.

"That her?" Mr. Knowles enquired, stealing an uncircumspect glance.

"Looks like it," Higgins acknowledged.

"White woman, eh?"

"She was," Higgins agreed. "Damn good-looking one, too. It's always the good-lookers who get bumped off; they cause all the trouble."

"Local gal?" asked Mr. Knowles, resisting the temptation to look again.

Higgins shrugged. "Don't think so—face like that would be remembered. Hard to say, of course. In this place, people come and go."

"Not European women, though," Mr. Knowles commented.

"No, not European women. 'Course, she could have been a Chilli," Superintendent Higgins reflected. "Can't always tell until they open their mouths, and as is to be expected, there's nothing in this bag that helps," he murmured, gently sifting through the small pile on his handkerchief. "Ah well, dare say we'll soon find out."

"Why was she hacked up?" Mr. Knowles asked gruffly, wishing he hadn't mentioned it. The jagged ends of the neck had given him quite a turn.

"Easier carrying small parcels about than lugging a whole body," said Higgins from long experience. "Which indicates, of course, that the bits were brought up here to be disposed of. Not where she was done away with—site of murder elsewhere, lots of blood." He sounded pleased with himself.

"Sacrifice," Mistri suddenly mumbled. "White woman, very important sacrifice to Kali, terrible disaster will now be averted."

"What's he on about?" asked Higgins.

"Had too much to drink," Mr. Knowles said uneasily. "Not used to booze." All this talk of sacrifice was very disturbing; everyone was aware of the pagan undercurrents running so close to the surface. A thousand years of the Raj would probably never erase them.

Finally, Superintendent Higgins was satisfied he would learn no more from the witnesses, the location, or the victim, and the dismembered body was wrapped in a tarpaulin to be carted off to the hospital, where it would be further contemplated.

"Good Lord," said Mr. Knowles. "M'wife will be worried, long past breakfast, never stayed out this late before."

"Me, I am going to temple, make sacrifice of atonement," Mistri announced mournfully. "Very bad happenings."

"My God," said Mr. Knowles. "Atonement? D'you mean to say—?"

Mistri burped and tripped over a rock on the path down

from the reservoir. "Goat meat not good for fishing, gods most dissatisfied with Mistri, stick head of white woman on his hook. Ayee, I am most unworthy person."

"What about me?" Knowles said rationally. "I caught a bit of her, too, didn't I? But I fished with rice soaked in beer, nothing blasphemous about that."

"Ayee, sa'b, you come to temple, too, make much atonement."

"Don't think Mrs. Knowles will go for that," said Mr. Knowles, harrumphing. "She's quite keen on the Church of England and all that."

The church bells were ringing. For the first time in many years, the C. of E. bells were late; but the faithful merely thought their clocks must be wrong and adjusted them accordingly. The R.C. bell had tinkled on time, but it was assumed, by the Protestants, that it was early.

"Got further to come, the Catholics," declared Mrs. Fitter Jones. "On the outskirts of town, they all live, not in the better district like us."

"But, still, unlike them it is to be early," said Mrs. Darsi Jones. "Wonder what's up?"

Mrs. Knowles hurried to catch up with them, her face important with the dreadful news she was carrying. "There's been a murder!" she cried. "My husband found the body— a female—in the reservoir it was, all chopped up in little pieces."

"Oh my, gracious me!" exclaimed Mrs. Darsi Jones. "A murder, is it?"

"Wonder if she was an R.C.?" queried Mrs. Fitter Jones, as if that answered one riddle at least.

"Who was it?" asked Mrs. Barhill, who had just caught up with them all and instantly understood the gist of the conversation.

"A stranger," said Mrs. Knowles. "White, but probably a chee-chee since no one has reported a European missing, and according to Inspector Higgins she'd been in the water several days."

"Several days?" cried Mrs. Barhill. "Oh Lord, I feel sick! To think that we—"

Aghast, they all stared at each other.

"I hope she wasn't diseased," said Mrs. Knowles. "But you can't tell with Chilli-cracks."

Jane and Mary strolled behind their elders, heads together. They had a lot to talk about.

"To think that up there, while we were riding around below with one of the Virgins...!" Mary relished.

"Will it be safe to go on our walk there after lunch?" Jane shuddered.

"Oh, yes," Mary grinned. "Don't worry, we're going to have an escort."

Jane looked hastily towards her mother, but Mrs. Barhill was deep in conversation with her cronies. "Who?" Jane asked.

"Four nice young men," Mary said airily. "Just dying to meet you, they are."

"Where did you find them?" Jane asked suspiciously. She was wondering whether to confide in Mary that she had fallen in love with the true King of Ireland that morning.

"They're new apprentices—pukka sa'bs—Special Grade."

"My father'll kill me—" Jane said doubtfully.

"He'll never know," said Mary with assurance. "He'll think you're having tea with Mother and me and practising dance-steps. And what the eye doesn't see—" She broke off and grinned.

"Well—" said Jane, her heart beginning to pound. MacNamara had said he would see her there that afternoon, in the very same place on the Maidan; he had ignored her protests, laughed at her stuttering denials. "I'll see you, my Queen!" he had declared, leaping into the saddle and wheeling off.

"I'll see you, my Queen!" The words were music in her ears.

Arriving at the church, Jane looked about hopefully for someone to tell her what to play. There appeared to be some degree of confusion this morning. It seemed that the temporary vicar, the Reverend Morgan Morgan, had spent the entire night praying in his garden, and was now fast asleep. She approached Mr. Edwards, who this morning was not himself. Why, positively untidy he looked, Jane thought, amazed.

"Any idea of the hymns or the psalms?" she asked.

"Play what you like," he said.

"I can't do that," Jane protested. "The new vicar may have something prepared to go with his sermon."

"I doubt it," said Mr. Edwards. "I don't think he knows what the words planning or preparation mean." He ran his fingers through his hair, causing it to stick up in tufts. "I know," he said, inspired. "Last week's numbers are still up. Play them—no one will even notice."

As the church began to fill with its usual worthies, and a few unworthies, Jane played "Jesu, Joy of Man's Desiring," humming the words to herself. Her mind drifted off into a dream filled with a fair-haired, blue-eyed Irishman and a world where no paternal inspections, orders, or regulations existed. Suddenly she realized that all eyes had turned expectantly towards the altar.

The Reverend Morgan Morgan stood there. Jane waited, hands on keys, but the Reverend broke into a chant. "How beautiful are thy feet . . . the joints of thy thighs are like jewels . . . thy navel is like a round goblet which wanteth not liquor . . ."

Slowly, the congregation began to sit down.

"What's he on about?" muttered Mrs. Maughan. "Must be chapel."

The voice chanted on, "Thy belly is like an heap of wheat set about with lilies . . . thy two breasts are like two young roes that are twins. . . . Oh, Avril, my Avril . . . Come, my beloved, let us go forth into the field . . ."

"The man's quite mad," said Miss Blenkinsop icily, while Miss Toogood gasped and struggled to compose herself.

"Let us sing," the Reverend Morgan Morgan suddenly announced. The congregation struggled to its feet and Jane struck the opening bars of "To Be a Pilgrim." Before the verse could begin, the Reverend Morgan Morgan broke into a completely different tune in a strong voice, in an unknown language. His wonderful voice soared to the rafters.

The congregation sat down, baffled but spellbound. Deep sighs came from Mrs. Darsi Jones and Mrs. Fitter Jones as the last perfect note died away.

"Beautiful, it was," moaned Mrs. Darsi Jones. "Beautiful, like chapel."

The clergyman moved towards the pulpit, seemed to hesitate, then mounted. He stood swaying inside, looking over everyone with a beatific smile.

"I do not approve of the order of this service," Miss Blenkinsop hissed to Miss Harris. "I shall complain most strenuously to the Bishop."

Miss Toogood was staring at the Reverend Morgan Morgan in a trance.

"I am happy to be here," the clergyman said in his deep, rich voice. "Most happy. It is a beautiful spot." He paused, and as he continued, his voice deepened. "The winter is past, the rain has gone. The voice of the turtle is heard in the land." He paused again, and looked about him. "My theme is love. Love," he repeated. "There is not enough love, not enough trust. Love," he repeated again, almost conversationally, as he slipped to his knees.

The Honorable Bertram Papworth turned and glared at Mr. Edwards, church elder. "That man is drunk!" he almost shouted.

"Hush!" said Mr. Edwards. Something about Morgan Morgan rang a deep chord within him.

"Yes, hush," said the Reverend Morgan Morgan, putting one finger on his lips. He slipped slowly from view, and then laboriously pulled himself onto his knees again, so that only his head showed, tortoise-like, above the rim of the box. "As I was saying . . . love one another . . . love is the sweetest thing . . ."

Suddenly Miss Toogood was on her feet, hands clasped before her, face white with panic. She opened her mouth, and the most incredible music poured out. Clear and true, a beautiful soprano soared and swooped through the church like the sound of an angel in heaven. A Welsh heaven.

On his knees at first, then slowly staggering upright, the Reverend Morgan Morgan joined in, and together they made the music of the Valleys.

There was a long, astounded silence; and then the Reverend Morgan Morgan held out his arms as wide as they would go, his face radiant.

"Avril!" he cried.

"Morgan!" Miss Toogood uttered. "I thought you were dead."

"Wonderful, it is," Mrs. Darsi Jones sighed. "Just like home, isn't it?"


$M$r. Edwards walked slowly back to "The Cedars." He was a very troubled man. Lizzie had not recovered as he had so confidently expected; far from it, she had built a nest in the corner of her room and tweeted frantically whenever he approached her.

"She thinks you're going to stand on her eggs," said Mrs. Edwards.

"Don't be so silly, she hasn't got any eggs," he said crossly.

"Yes she has—six," said Mrs. Edwards coolly. "Blue, like a thrush's, very pretty they are, too."

Sonny was no help, either. No one had seen him for days, although there were some completely unbelievable rumours flying about concerning him and that sluttish Mrs. Ray. And as for Claire, instead of standing by her husband (and therefore his family), she had gone running off home to her mother.

And then there was Maisie. You'd think he could depend on his youngest and quietest child, but no! Not only had she declared her intention of marrying an R.C., but rumour had it that there was more than the hint of the tarbrush in his family—black kids she'd be dropping; not even the ornate iron gates (replicas of the Hertfordshire ones) would keep them out of the family tree in the big Bible. Little black Chillis, his grandchildren, littering the lawns, muddying up the natural order of things. Bad show.

Faced with an astounding revelation, Mr. Edwards stopped in the middle of the pavement.

"Love," he said loudly. He stared up at the black Queen Victoria's sneering face. "Love!"

That was what all the trouble was about, that was why God was frowning so dreadfully upon him. He did not know love. He was greedy and selfish, clutching his wealth to his bosom, wanting it only for himself, and some for his family.

"The voice of the turtle is heard in the land . . . love one another . . . love is the sweetest thing . . ." a plangent echo in his soul.

"Love!" he shouted exultantly. "Love!"

He entered his house at a run, spinning his hat across the hall to the hat-stand, tossing his cane at the tall blue-and-white-glazed umbrella stand. The cane missed and pierced a glass-fronted what-not in a splintering of dangerous shards.

Mrs. Edwards, who had not attended church since Lizzie had become a bird, came running out of the drawing-room.

"Mrs. Edwards, you will be the first to know. I am giving away all my money. Everything. Stocks, shares, pension fund, the lot."

Mrs. Edwards stood stock still and stared at him. "It was only a matter of time," she said quite casually.

"Verily I say unto you, that a rich man shall hardly enter into the kingdom of heaven," Mr. Edwards declared, removing his jacket and loosening his tie.

"I don't think God intends you to give up your pension fund, dear," Mrs. Edwards said mildly. "You have to have something for your old age."

"And again I say unto you, it is easier for a camel to go through the eye of a needle, than for a rich man to enter into the kingdom of God." He took off his collar and removed the studs from his shirt.

"Are you getting completely undressed out in the hall?" Mrs. Edwards wanted to know. "Retiring for the night, perhaps?"

Mr. Edwards ignored her question. "Send the mali to find the durzi-wallah," he said. "I want some simple, holy garments made. I shall travel through the highways and the byways distributing money to the poor."

"Hmm, get yourself murdered, you mean," said Mrs. Edwards. "If you want to give your money away, give it to the Zenana Mission—perhaps they need another motor-car. Meanwhile, come and have lunch. Roast lamb with mint sauce. We were going to have those pheasants Jamie Jameson sent over, but Lizzie got upset. She's been very sensitive ever since she laid her eggs."


$M$r. and Mrs. Nightingale had been invited to lunch with the Papworths. Mrs. Nightingale, great friend and confidante of Miss Blenkinsop, was the daughter of an Anglican bishop; but even her Christian charity and fortitude was wont to crumble before the ordeal of a Papworth luncheon.

"Must you drink, dear?" she questioned her husband. "That's the third Tom Collins you've had since church."

"Nothing wrong with Tom Collins," he replied. "Mostly Schweppes, only a splash of gin."

"And must you pretend to agree with everything that dreadful girl has to say?"

"Have to swallow it, along with their inevitable brown stew and caramel custard," said Mr. Nightingale grimly.

"Strange, how all he wants to eat is nursery food," mused Mrs. Nightingale. "Something odd there."

"Probably seduced by his governess," said Mr. Nightingale. "The proverbial hand-reared boy, what?"

"Really!" said Mrs. Nightingale primly.

"Well, thank God these summons from the big white chief happen only once a quarter—a bit like the vicar getting invited to lunch by the bishop."

"A most unfortunate comparison," said Mrs. Nightingale. "And quite unnecessary to invoke the Lord's name."

Mr. Nightingale sighed. "I wish it was easier than it is, but Mr. Papworth is a senior member of the Railway Board, which is made up of many Papworths. If I am to progress I can only do so by keeping them all sweet, and if that means eating brown stew and caramel custard, then I *love* it!"

Mrs. Nightingale got the last word in. "But it doesn't mean that you have to kowtow to Vivien Papworth. She is nothing else but a vulgar tart with a silver spoon. She'll come to a bad end, mark my words." In Mrs. Nightingale's world, bad girls always came to bad ends; they deserved nothing better.

They could have walked across their adequate lawns, through a high rhododendron hedge (gloriously in bloom) and over the Honourable Bertram's perfect lawns, but somehow that was too casual, and not encouraged by the Papworths. Instead, dressed in their best, bearer carrying a parasol, they walked. Down their driveway, a few yards along the King's Road, and up Papworth's very grand carriage-drive to his very grand house.

They were shown into the drawing room, the one overlooking the front lawns with a distant view of the Seven Sisters. Mr. Nightingale sighed as he seated himself. He had noted the bare board in the adjoining dining-room and the complete absence of the uniformed bearers.

Lucky if they got a meal before tea-time, and Lord, was he hungry. He sighed again, and hoped his stomach wouldn't rumble. He should have had a quick beef sandwich and a glass of milk. The drinks he had consumed were making him sleepy. With an effort he opened his eyes as the Honourable Bertram and Mrs. Papworth came in.

Mrs. Papworth seated herself next to Mrs. Nightingale and flashed her false teeth at her. "You don't drink, m'dear, good." Turning to Mr. Nightingale, she demanded, "What's this about the 'Prentices' Ball, hear you've made a mess of it?"

Aargh! Mr. Nightingale wanted to shriek out. Instead he smiled and said, "Um, no, actually, it's—"

"I was only saying to Vivien this morning, can't have that—can't have the 'Prentices' Ball mucked up, Board won't like it at all, Papworth won't like it either, will you, dear?" she boomed.

Mr. Papworth was pouring himself a drink, a large, warm gin. He glared ferociously down the length of the room. "Heads will roll, heads will roll."

Nightingale sighed. "There is no mess, everything is in order. I spent some time with Les Topping this morning, and he's got it all in hand. Then I saw Mrs. Knowles; the bakery will turn out all the delicacies, they will be as excellent as always. She informed me that Mr. Knowles is off to Calcutta on Tuesday to see to the ordering of the spirits, novelties, confectionery."

"Why didn't you talk to Mr. Knowles?" Mrs. Papworth wanted to know. "I should have thought you'd have made a point of it."

"He was busy—tied up with some murder."

The Papworths and Mrs. Nightingale stared at Mr. Nightingale.

"Murder?" said Mr. Papworth. "What murder?"

"You didn't tell me," said Mrs. Nightingale accusingly.

"Who's he done in?" said Mrs. Papworth.

"Apparently he found a hacked-up body in the reservoir—fished it out on the end of his hook instead of a fish."

"Good Lord!" exclaimed Mrs. Nightingale, then blushed, wondering what her father, the bishop, would say if he heard her.

"Hope it doesn't interfere with the ball," said Mr. Papworth, swilling his gin and pouring another.

"Do they know who it was?" asked Mrs. Papworth.

"Not yet, although Inspector Higgins reckons he'll soon

have it solved. Not that easy bumping someone off, especially a European, and getting away with it."

Vivien Papworth strolled into the room, stared at the occupants, and yawned. "Lord, what a bore," she said to nobody in particular. Lighting her inevitable cigarette, she blew a stream of smoke into Mrs. Nightingale's face.

Mrs. Nightingale coughed delicately and said, "So bad for your lungs, my dear."

Vivien glanced at her, surprised, and blew out another stream. "Talking about the boring old ball, God, how tedious."

Mr. Nightingale smiled ingratiatingly. "This year, we hope to have a bit more—er—style. Just what you wanted, an Arabian Nights theme."

"Sounds more like it," said Vivien. "Fancy dress, h'm?"

Mindful of what Topping had told him, Nightingale said cautiously, "Well, within reason, what? No belly dancers, ha ha."

Vivien dangled one leg over the arm of a chair. "What fun," she said. "I think I'll go as an houri. I must drop in and ask the Rajah what an houri looks like; he might have some costume or another." She glanced sideways at Mrs. Nightingale. "You could go as a dancing girl, gold breastplates and a jewel in your navel; the apprentices would be all over you."

Mrs. Nightingale blushed scarlet and looked at her husband for help, but smiling foolishly, he was looking away.

Vivien rose, yawned, and stretched like a cat. She walked up to Mr. Nightingale and smiled into his eyes. "And what about you?" she purred. "You'd make a lovely sheik."

Mrs. Papworth laughed richly. "You are a naughty girl, Viv. Don't tease Mr. Nightingale, he won't enjoy his lunch."

"Talking of lunch, I'm late for an appointment at the Officers' Club," said Vivien, floating towards the door. "Toodle-oo."

Christ, there goes lunch, thought Mr. Nightingale. They never bother to eat when she's not around to stir their stumps. I'm starving, don't think I can hold out much longer. His stomach rumbled, and he coughed to hide the noise.

Mrs. Papworth launched into a discussion of Les Topping's forthcoming production of *The Belle of New York*, in which she thought Vivien should have the lead, while Mr. Papworth stared morosely into his gin. Mrs. Nightingale stared in front of her, her mind wandering to the time when her husband would be a big Railway boss and she would entertain, put her guests at ease and feed them well.

"A good roast and apple pie, none of this brown stew," she heard herself say, and suddenly realised she had spoken aloud. She looked about wildly, hoping no-one had heard. To her despair, they were all staring at her.

Mr. Nightingale rose to his feet with alacrity, a fevered gleam in his eyes. "Jolly good show," he said, galloping towards the door. "I'm starving."

Superintendent Higgins strode into the Institute, long steps making an impressive ring on the marble floors, two sergeants trotting with him.

"Babu," he called loudly. "Babu, ko hai!"

He banged impatiently on the bar door. Babu opened the door a crack and peered out. "Not opening time, sahib." He made to shut the door.

"Just a second." Higgins expertly slipped his foot in the crack. "Where's Topping sahib?"

"Resting, sahib. Not feeling fine today, stomach most bad."

"Well, go and fetch him, police business. I want to see the pair of you."

Babu shrugged. "Topping sahib in his rooms—why not come with me, sahib? Saving journey, going all that way and coming back down again."

"You're a lazy devil," said Higgins. "Beats me how you don't get fat, all that sitting around boozing."

Babu looked scandalised. "Me drink? No, sahib. Religion forbid drinking and smoking. I only sell to sahibs for Institute—never touch the demned stuff."

"Oh, all right, all right," said Higgins cheerfully. "Lead the way."

Babu climbed the stairs, muttering under his breath. He knocked on the door. "Topping sahib, it is the police superintendent coming to see you."

There was no sound from within. Babu knocked again. "Topping sahib, Superintendent sahib."

There was a shuffling noise; then Topping opened the door slowly. He looked sicker than a dog, thought Higgins; no stamina, these boyish handsome types. A few late nights, a bug in their drinking water, and they keel over like flies sprayed with Flit.

"What are we supposed to have done?" Topping muttered.

Higgins laughed. "Why do people think we're about to make an arrest every time we show our faces? Fact is, want to have a word with you, old chap; need your help."

Topping managed an awful grin and moved aside. "Never a moment's peace, not even on a Sunday. Well, what can we do for you?"

"Thanks, I will," said Higgins, sitting down and looking about him. "Nice place you've got up here, very private it must be."

"When you've got a job like mine, dealing with hordes of people all day and half the night, you need some peace and quiet, somewhere you can get away from it all."

"Quite, quite. Very nice just the same."

Topping and Babu stood looking at him. The two sergeants lined themselves up by the door. Topping began to feel uncomfortable; he knew these casual types—like smiling crocodiles, they were. Very sharp teeth.

"Have a murder on my hands," Higgins started. "I say, old chap, are you all right?"

"Stomach out, need a drink," Topping muttered, stumbling to a chair. Babu ran into the bathroom and emerged with some fizzing Andrew's Liver Salts in a glass.

"Making you feel better, sahib, clean you right out, like brush in drain."

Topping took the glass and gulped greedily.

"As I was saying," continued Higgins, "I have a murder on my hands. Strangled and chopped up, not very pleasant."

"Ari," said Babu, "that is not good; there is much nastiness in the bazaar, much killing."

"I don't think this has anything to do with the bazaar," said Higgins. "White woman, handsome once, young. Knowles found her, thinks she is a stranger. He knows most of the European types from around here. Says he has never seen her before. Well, somebody must have seen her, and somebody must have known her well enough to strangle her, then chop her up and dump all the bits in the reservoir."

"The reservoir, uri, uri," said Babu, rolling his eyes towards Topping. "No wonder you are being so sick, sahib."

"Why do you say that?" Higgins asked, narrowing his eyes.

"Topping sahib drink much water, also swim much, say water very cleansing, but I am thinking water with body in it not so very healthy."

"I don't think a body would make that much difference to the quality of the reservoir water, full of weeds and fish and Lord knows what else," said Higgins. "Anyway, you boil your drinking water, don't you?"

"Mali lazy," Babu proclaimed.

"Well, let's get on with my business," said Higgins impatiently. "This place is pretty central. We want a notice on all the notice boards and displayed outside, with a photograph—"

"Photograph?" Topping asked, apprehension seizing him.

"In her handbag. Not much else in it of any use, as could be predicted, but no doubt about it being her." Higgins shook his head. "Very nasty—but you can't have a body in the water for four or five days without some signs of wear and tear. Anyway, we've got a picture. Everybody comes here; someone is bound to recognise her, or at least tell us who she was with, you know, the kind of information we want." He looked at Topping. "Well, what about it?"

Topping put a shaking hand to his mouth. "Very awkward," he said. "You have picked an impossible time. It's the Apprentices' Ball in a few days; we're decorating everything, taking down all the notice boards. Persian garden," he explained vaguely.

"Too bad," said Higgins. "This is police business. Comes first, I'm afraid. Boards will have to stay up. And I don't see why we can't have a notice by the gates. Not turning *them* into a Persian garden, are you?"

"Yes, yes," Topping improvised wildly. "Sheik's tents over each of the gates. Papworth won't like it at all," he added as a clincher. "Mixing up murder with the Ball, gives J.M.P. and the Railway a bad name." He appealed to Babu. "Can't have police notices all over the place, can we?"

Babu agreed. "Most disturbing, it will be. Photograph of dead woman and many flowers, look like funeral, not like dance." Suddenly he brightened. "Bar will not be Persian garden; notice can go there, many people are using the bar."

"Good," said Higgins. "That's settled then."

Jane jumped on her new green Raleigh and went spinning down Prince's Road, Ayah puffing away behind her on her big black old bone-shaker. Higgins, leaving the gates of the Institute, smiled as he saw Jane's shining auburn hair blowing in the breeze.

"Ah, well," he said to his two disciples. "Nice to be young and carefree."

"Hello," said Mary, coming out onto the steps of her parents' house and smiling down at Jane. "You look pretty chirpy."

"I was in a blue funk in case Father came home and put the kibosh on me leaving the house," Jane confessed.

"Thought he may have heard about the murder at the reservoir and all that. A white woman! He'll be convinced it's a rape case and I'm next on the list."

"The murder wasn't *at* the reservoir, silly," said Mary, leading the way into the house. "Inspector Higgins said the killer lugged her up there and threw her bits in. Anyway, he wouldn't be hanging around up there now, would he?"

"I suppose not," Jane agreed, then stopped dead as she stared at four attractive young men who rose politely as she walked into the sitting room.

Mary grinned. "Ma decided that we'd better have our escort right from the front door, so to speak. Robert and Andrew McIntosh, Freddy Payne, John Brown."

The young men bowed gravely, and although they looked charmingly boyish and friendly, Jane felt uncomfortable. Thanks to her father, she had never met enough boys her own age to feel at ease with them, but at least she didn't automatically assume that they would leap upon her and start raping her, which was the conviction her father had tried to instil in her.

She need not have worried; within a very few minutes, with Mary being her usual natural self, and with the boys chatting as amiably as if she were one of their sisters or an old school chum, Jane found herself completely relaxed.

"You're pretty keen on Robert, aren't you?" she murmured to Mary as they set off on their walk, Ayah like a black shadow shuffling along behind.

"Does it show?"

"Well, it certainly shows that he's crazy about you. You're a fast worker—they only arrived last week."

"What d'you think of him?"

"He's very young. I mean, it's not serious, is it?"

"Could be," said Mary. "His father practically owns the Railway, even old Papworth answers to him. He and Andrew are being trained to take over one day. Just think," she teased, "I could be queen bee."

They cut across the Maidan, and all of a sudden, he

was there; his Arab's hooves thundering, mane tossing. He was leading another horse. Side-saddle.

"Good heavens!" Mary exclaimed as he leapt from his horse and tossed Jane up; light as a feather, she seemed, eyes wide, leg hooked over the pommel.

"Jane, where are you going?" Mary called as Jane and the true King of Ireland wheeled and thundered off to the hills.

"To see the world," Jane cried. "To the halls of Tara."

Mary stared after her. She looked at the four young apprentices. "I don't think I should walk with you by myself," she said, somewhat confused. "Perhaps we should go to the Institute, play tennis or something?"

"Ayah no chase after missie baba, all way to the Institute, Ayah too old. Ayah chaperone very good Missie Mary. We walk, okay?" Ayah said, suddenly coming to life.

Mary started to laugh. "I'd forgotten all about you, Ayah. Okay, we walk." After a while, she said to Robert, "Where *are* the halls of Tara?"

He sat easy in the saddle, born to ride. She had ridden little; all her years had been spent in school, but still, she bore herself well, back straight, hands loose. The air was clean, the sun warm but not too hot, a cooling scented wind blew from the heights.

They breasted a rise, and sat looking down on the town spread out below. The bright green of the Maidan, the silver sparkle of the reservoir, the snaking lines of the Railway. The marble Queen Victoria glowed in the light of the setting sun; almost translucent, she was.

"What are you doing here?" Jane finally asked. "I mean, what do you do?"

He inclined his head gravely. "I'm a gambling man."

Jane considered his words; she did not wish to pry. A movement over his left shoulder caught her attention. They were on a level with the black Queen Victoria's volcanic face. Her chin thrust out and curved in to form a neck, at the base of which were some scrubby thorns, which, from a distance, resembled the ruffles of her collar. The thorns parted, and Jane found herself staring straight into a tiger's amber eyes.

"I don't want to alarm you," she said, "but there's a tiger behind you, and it looks quite hungry."

"Well now, let's be looking at the cat," he said, turning his head casually. "You're right—it is hungry, but that goat it's eating should satisfy its hunger; and two tigers it is, not one."

"Two?" Jane tried not to sound nervous.

"Don't worry—what with the goat they're tearing to pieces and the sun in their eyes, I believe we'll be safe enough. But careful now—move off nice and easy."

With reins loose but muscles and heels in careful control, Jane and MacNamara walked their horses at a leisurely pace back down to the plain. He chatted lightly to her, describing his ancestral home in Ireland, a tumbledown castle in Shannon, and the fiery Queen Maeve of Connaught from whom his claim as King of Ireland was descended. He told her about Niall of the Nine Hostages, Strongbow, and Ruadri Ua Conchubair, known as Rory O'Connor; and the Norse and the Welsh and the English who had lusted after the green land; and the English who had won it. So beguiling was his voice, and so enchanting his tales, Jane forgot to be scared, and indeed when they arrived at the foot of the hill leading to the pumping station, she looked about her somewhat dazed.

Mary and the Apprentices had returned from their stroll through the sweet cork trees, and Mary had a glow about her not connected with the effort of her climb.

MacNamara bowed as he handed Jane over to the custody of her Ayah. "It wouldn't be a bad idea to go straight home," he said to Mary and the boys. "There seem to be two tigers up there on the slopes."

"Tigers!" Mary exclaimed. "Dad said he thought he heard one when he was fishing last night, but dismissed it as nonsense. Or whisky," she added.

"It was neither," said MacNamara firmly. He smiled into Jane's eyes. "It was the real thing."

Then he was mounting with a lithe swing, and with a polite nod to Mary, rode off in a soft jangle of silver bit. Jane stared after him, bemused. He had said nothing about seeing her again, nothing about where he was staying, beyond that passing reference to first seeing her in the Maharajah's palace, or what he was really doing in Jamalpur.

Was he prince charming—or was he the demon king? It didn't much matter; she had completely fallen under his spell.

The box-wallah was there when Jane arrived home, and somehow, in the anticipation of new clothes, tigers on the Seven Sisters did not seem too important. Besides, confiding the tale could lead to no end of complications. How would she explain what she was doing up in the hills in the first place?—and any allusion to her cavalier would more than likely bring the roof down.

The box-wallah lowered his box, and helped his coolie down with his. "Much fine nautch cuppra," he beamed, opening the first box carefully. From a heap of tissue-paper he lifted out a soft lace dress, not quite peach, not quite apricot; it was the charming colour of tea-roses, a perfect foil for Jane's bright hair, green eyes, and clear complexion.

Jane sighed and held out her hands. The lace cascaded over her arms and to the floor, armfuls of luxury. "It's beautiful," she breathed.

The box-wallah dug deeper, lifting out more tissue. Now he held up a sparkling silver gown, tight in the body, flaring out at the knees, backless, almost topless. Jane's eyes widened.

"Dad'll die," she said.

"We'll have both," said Mrs. Barhill calmly. "There'll be more dances this season. You'll knock 'em all into a hoop."

"Now, for memsahib, ranee they will be thinking you," said the box-wallah, opening the second box and pulling back layers of tissue-paper. "Very special, Woods mem make very special."

He held up a black lace dress and a silver slip. "Memsahib wear black dress, Missie wear silver dress, very nice, most complementary." Again, he bent down. "Another fine special," he said enticingly, holding up a soft brown and fawn crepe. "Very latest; Papworth memsahib wanting, but too fat."

"You mean," said Jane, "that Papworth memsahib turned it down."

"No, no, Missie, that not what I mean. Papworth mem not seeing very fine dress. She order, yes, very latest she be wanting, but she too fat, give Woods bad name. She squeeze and squeeze," he demonstrated, sucking in his waist and puffing out his chest. "Then everybody saying, where she get such bad-fitting dress, Woods no good. Barhill memsahib very fine figure, everybody saying Woods very good, make very nice dress."

"I'll take all four," said Mrs. Barhill, still as cool as a cucumber. "I've decided life's too short to get in a stew over your father, Jane. Leave me to take care of him."

Jane gaped, astonished.

"Besides," said Mrs. Barhill, turning quite pink, "I have something to tell you. I learnt this afternoon in a telegraph that my Aunt Nora has died." She smiled grimly. "Soon I will be a woman of independent means, so your father had better mind his p's and q's, or we'll be off."

"Poor Aunt Nora. It's terribly sad," Jane said slowly, unable to grasp the portent of the cold wind about to blow up her father's shirt-tail. She wished she could summon more regret for a relative she had never met, but whose letters from England had brought another world closer. "Poor Aunt Nora," she repeated, and sighed.

But Mrs. Barhill wasn't listening. "He who pays the piper, calls the tune," she said. "And from now on, the tune's on me." She picked up her purse and looked at the box-wallah. "How much down?" she asked with assurance.

\*　　　\*　　　\*

Night had fallen, dark, absolute.

Mrs. Briggs, venturing out with a hurricane lantern to check the safety of her beloved hens, dropped the lantern with a clatter, and galloping back to the safety of her bungalow, clutched at the snoozing form of her husband curled up on the sofa.

"Briggs, Briggs," she gabbled, shaking him violently. "There's a tiger out there."

"Wha's tha'—?" mumbled Briggs, from a ten-pint semi-coma.

"There's a tiger, a huge beast, in the back lane. I saw it clear as daylight, simply enormous, it was."

"Cobblers! You've been seeing things. I dare say—"

Before Briggs had completed his derisory sentence, a roar shattered the night, so close the windows shook.

"Bloody 'ell—what was that?" His mouth fell open as he struggled to sit up.

"I told you, a tiger. About ten feet long. I saw it in the back lane."

"Lock the door. Perhaps it will go away."

"What about my chickens?"

"If it eats the chickens, it won't eat us. Now lock the door."


In their servants' quarters, Chandhi was serving her lord with damn fine hot curry (green chillies, red chillies, most agreeable on a cool evening), plenty of dhal spiced up with caraway and cardamom seeds, and floury roti.

Solomon broke off a piece of roti, dipped it in the curry, curled it round into a little parcel and popped it into his mouth. His eyes rolled with approval. "Very fine cook thou art becoming, Chandhi."

Chandhi lowered her eyes modestly, offering him a bowl of fragrant lime water with small blossoms floating on the surface. Solomon dipped his fingers in, wiped them on a linen cloth, and drank his cha with gusto. As he ate again, he contemplated Chandhi. "Hast thou a child in thy belly yet?" he enquired. "A child of my loins to keep thee busy?"

Chandhi raised her eyes; a blush stained her round, moon face. "I cannot tell, my lord."

"Ayee, woman—is your body so different from other women's that you cannot tell such things?"

"Last moon, I was without child. This moon has not yet passed. I cannot tell."

"If it is barren you are, home wilt thou go, double quick time."

"And will my lord be returning my dowry?" she asked boldly.

"Uri, what kind of a woman are thou to speak so?" Solomon exclaimed, swelling with wrath.

Chandhi did not answer, and, muttering, Solomon consumed the rest of his meal, washed his fingers, then stood up. "Come—do your duty. Tonight I will be planting a child in thy belly. Seven nights have I held back from thy bed to strengthen my essence. Now it is strong, a fat man-child will you be giving me. There will be no more talk of sending you back to your father's house."

Chandhi salaamed and started clearing the bowls away. "Leave them, leave them," Solomon exclaimed, removing his silken belt.

"But my lord, we will have rats in our quarters," Chandhi protested. "Let me put them outside at least."

Solomon pulled her close, his hot breath fanning the oiled muskiness of her throat. "Later, later," he muttered. "Come, remove thy sari, your lord desires you. Ayee, such a heaviness I have. Make haste, lest I spill my seed on the ground and not inside thee."

Obediently, Chandhi started to unbutton his achkan and untied the cord of his pantaloons. She wriggled out of her sari and within moments Solomon had pushed her onto her pallet and was thrusting in ecstasy, invoking the blessings of all the goddesses on his efforts. His panting had almost peaked when a loud roar sounded from without.

Chandhi screamed and twisted away from under him.

"Shaitan!" Solomon swore violently, oblivious to all external stimuli in the moment of his passion. "On the ground, on the ground!"

"Lord—" cringed Chandhi, looking towards the doorway.

"Thou hast brought such disaster! Back to your father will you be going in the morning, ayee, and I will be keeping thy dowry for my pains."

"Lord, what was that noise?" Chandhi whispered, her eyes frantic in the glow of the oil lamp.

"Noise? I heard no noise," Solomon cried furiously, climbing to his feet. "Uri-mia—I will be beating you most violently after you have washed my person. Such a thing never have I known of, a wife who refuses her lord's sacred essence! Uri, such complaining will I be making to your father, such shame he will feel."

Another great roar sounded closer by, and Solomon shrivelled.


Mr. and Mrs. Knowles had eaten dinner and were now playing gin rummy with Mary. The room was mellow with the light of oil lamps.

Mrs. Knowles raised her head. "What was that?" she asked.

They all stared at each other; then Mary got up and gazed out of the window towards the back of the house.

"My God, it's a tiger," she said. "It's come down from the hills. My God, I don't believe it."

As she spoke, there was an ear-splitting roar, and she screamed, backing away from the window. Mr. Knowles jumped up, knocking over the card table, and hurried over to the window, his wife on his heels. Together, using the curtains as some kind of a shield, they peered out.

"Can't see a thing," whispered Mrs. Knowles.

"Must have gone round the back, towards the servants' quarters."

They stared at each other.

"Better go for the police—or Jameson," said Mr. Knowles. "He'll know how to deal with it—tigers are his cup of tea."

"You can't go out there!" Mrs. Knowles was aghast.

"Have to. Servants can't face down a tiger—they're practically at its mercy."

Even as he spoke, there was a spine-chilling scream, ending in a long-drawn-out gurgling.

"What was that?" Mrs. Knowles gasped.

A roar answered her. She and Mr. Knowles tumbled back, and the curtain pole gave way and crashed to the floor. Mary screamed, fully expecting the tiger to come leaping through the window. But there was a long silence, then a pattering of feet. An agitated scrabbling at the door.

They all froze and stared at one another. Mr. Knowles called out almost inaudibly, "Ko hai, who's there?"

"Sahib, sahib, bhag, bhag."

Mrs. Knowles staggered to his feet and opened the door a fraction as Solomon and Chandhi, clutching the sheet her lord was wearing, slipped through. Their eyes were rolling white in their heads.

"Sa'b, two tigers." Solomon held his arms stretched out. "Big, big tigers, making big noise, oh, truly terrible to see. Pheelip not making sing along, dance no more. No more making eyes at Chandhi, no more making love to other women, Pheelip tiger meat."

Chandhi started moaning, rocking back and forth on her haunches. She had somehow swathed her sari about her in their flight from their quarters, and now she pulled the end over her head, exposing half her buttocks.

"Uri-mia," Solomon swore. "Cover thy shameful body, woman."

Mr. Knowles cleared his throat. "Was that Philip we heard just now?"

"Pheelip protecting dhobi's woman. She outside, make chappati. Tiger smell, want to eat, dhobi woman not willing to share her lord's dinner, so tiger eat her. Pheelip he throw hot stones at tiger, tiger not happy, eat Pheelip also."

"Oh dear, this is dreadful," said Mrs. Knowles. "I can't believe it."

"Tigers gone now I'm thinking," said Solomon, sitting on his haunches, adjusting the sheet. "Solomon open door little crack, see tigers going, tails going swish, swish." He rocked on his heels.

"Gone where?" asked Mrs. Knowles.

Solomon pointed vaguely into space. "Gone from compound, maybe along of hospital, maybe along of reservoir, maybe along of—"

"All right," said Mr. Knowles. "We'd better go and see what we can do for Philip and that poor woman."

Solomon rolled his eyes. "Not helping anyone now. Sahib, mem, stay here. Not know with tigers, maybe hiding. Solomon stay, guard you. Pheelip very dead. Dhobi woman not moving much, also."

"We can't just stay here," said Mrs. Knowles.

"Why not?" said Mr. Knowles, setting up the card table and gathering all the scattered cards. "Not much we can do out there, Solomon's right, and what's the point of getting torn to shreds? Won't do any good. Now whose deal is it?"


After brooding for a week, old Mrs. Jameson decided it was time she took the battle into her daughter-in-law's court. Summoning her ayah, she arrayed herself in her rusty black taffeta and sallied forth, eyes grim.

She didn't tell Jessie where she was going. Jessie had been barricaded in her room for days, emerging only when necessary, and the lord knew what she was up to in there with Dr. Ray. Sighs and moans. Strange silences. Soft laughter.

Mrs. Jameson had listened, her ears pressed up to the door, and filthy it was. Filthy. She compressed her lips. She had always known her daughter was no good; girls were no good. Give her sons any day. When the chips were down boys stuck with their mothers, the women who had borne them, the women who had suckled them. James would give her the loyalty she was due, and Miss Armstrong had better look out.

"Miss Armstrong, look out!" she said with great satisfaction, banging the floor with her stick as they left the house and she was carefully wheeled down the ramp from the veranda and out to the road.

"Faster!" she cried.

The road was dark, badly lit and full of pot-holes. Ayah grumbled, but Mrs. Jameson's blood was up; a battle song coursed through her veins. She rehearsed all she would say to Miss Armstrong.

In his usual condition, Jim Dale was half sprawled, half sitting against a wall on Jamie Jameson's veranda. He had turned up there, having exhausted all other supplies, pockets to let, to scrounge a drink and maybe a bed for the night. His daughter refused to let him in until he sobered up, but Jameson was a good sort, never one to turn his chums away.

Dale had not expected to find a new young wife established; a virago of a wife, a fishwife of a wife.

While Jameson had grinned weakly at him from the wings, the virago had bodily ejected Dale. She didn't say much, just flung him out and slammed the door.

Phew, he thought in his befuddled state, who needs a wife like that? Thank Christ I'm not married. Daughter's bad enough, but a wife. Phew!

He felt a hot breath fanning his face. Christ, was she back?

"Not interested," he mumbled, "Go 'way."

Most of his suit was ripped off and he received an enormous cuff that sent him flying off the veranda. He landed in some sweet jasmine bushes and heard them crackling and breaking as he sunk to the soft, loamy soil underneath. Hope there aren't any snakes or scorpions, he thought; then he passed out.

Inside the bungalow, Jameson and his wife had just

retired to bed when they heard a roar and a loud crashing.

"I can't believe it," said Miss Armstrong angrily. "He's broken in."

But in a blinding flash, Jameson realized what it was. "It's the female, after her cubs. She's scented them here."

"If you'd given them to that Barhill girl as you promised me—"

"Her father wouldn't allow it. Anyway, no use in crying over spilt milk; we've got them, and a tigress is roaming around the house somewhere. If we keep still, it will take the cubs and go."

"Shoot her!" Miss Armstrong screamed.

"Can't—you gave my guns away, remember?"

She stared at him, her mouth open.

Jameson got up and padded over to the window. He stared out. "She's leaving, got a cub in her mouth," he said after a few minutes.

Miss Armstrong stared at him, "Only one cub? Why not both?"

"Can only carry one. It'll be back for the other. Maybe in an hour or so—depends on where it's holed up."

"Very well, I shall drown the other, and while I'm doing that, you will find a gun and shoot it when it returns."

"That's not right, can't go around drowning cubs," Jameson protested, but she glared at him and marched out of the room, fire in her eyes.

Her blood-curdling screams filled the house. Jameson froze as he recognised the mauling snarls of a tiger. Seizing a chair, he ran to the hall and into the spare bedroom where the cubs had been kept. His wife was lying in a pool of blood on the floor, and a large tiger was leaping through the window with the remaining cub in its maw.

"Must have been two of 'em," he muttered professionally as he knelt by his wife's side. She was quite dead, her neck broken.

"Jamie, Jamie, where's my boy?" came his mother's quavering voice from the veranda. "Jamie, I thought I saw a tiger, must be seeing things. See how you've upset me, getting married like that. No consideration. My nerves—"

"Oh God! Mother!" he said, and stood up.

He heard the wheels of her chair creaking as the Ayah rolled it along the hall, heard his mother still complaining. Then she was in the doorway. She stared at his wife's mangled body, then at him.

"I knew Miss Armstrong was not for you," she said. "Better come home with your mother."

# THE
# THIRD
# SUNDAY

Saturday evening, the night of the ball, had at last arrived.

The Institute magically had been transformed into a Persian garden, perfumed, sparkling, flower-garlanded, lantern hung, alluring. Striped pavillions on velvety lawns; silk cushions, soft rugs. Main pathways carpeted. Graceful bowers of flowers, caged birds; strutting peacocks, very fine feathers, peacocks, but what a noise, and watch out, they like to peck mem's legs, tear silk stockings.

Veranda on the side of ballroom transformed into harem, place for ladies to giggle and gossip, catch breath, hide from pestiferous men. Silk carpets, piled cushions, low tables, settees, soft lights, very nice retreat for memsahibs, missie sa'bs. The double doors facing Victoria Street opened wide, make another room, very fine pavillion; lavish, luxurious as is befitting big bosses of the Railway. Private room for Sir Ian McIntosh, big-big boss of the Railway; the Very Honourable Bertram Papworth, next in line big boss; and most important guests. The stage curved toward toilets and dressing rooms like crescent moon, most unusual shape. Band from Calcutta, fancy dress like sheiks of Araby, muscles flexing, hair polished, teeth flashing.

As for the ballroom—uri bab, the ballroom—

"Breathtaking," sighed Mrs. Knowles, "Ab-so-lutely breathtaking."

"Splendid, splendid," boomed Mr. Nightingale, vigorously pumping Les Topping by the hand. "Jolly good show." Satisfied, he returned home to escort his wife.

In the ballroom, the Apprentices had surpassed themselves. The walls were painted to represent desert scenes and oases. The lights in the ceiling writhed in rainbow hues; twisted garlands of flowers and strands of crepe paper were looped to make a mosaic pattern like an inner court of the Alhambra. The floor had been polished brighter than a crystal, reflecting everything. "Like dancing on the water of the oasis itself," breathed Mrs. Knowles, as she surveyed the room for one final time.

Babu, resplendent in spotless, full, very pleated dhoti, with a gold embroidered waistcoat covering a bright red silk shirt, busied himself with polishing glasses, counting bottles, polishing imaginary dust from counters. Worrying.

The library had been converted into a buffet, decorated as an eastern café. The tables gleamed with spotless white linen cloths and starched, fluted linen napkins. Solomon was regal in his head bearer's uniform, the silver of his Railway badge in wide belt and puggaree shone and glistened with much polishing. Mrs. Knowles, in evening frock, was sitting at a trestle table, flushed, sipping a welcome cup of tea.

Resplendent in full evening dress, Mr. Knowles glanced at his watch. "Not long to go, you've done us proud, Mother." His eyes fell on the laden trestle tables, piled high with delicacies. "Best show I've seen in years—go far to get pastries like yours. Blumes are not anywhere up to your standard."

"Not been easy," said Mrs. Knowles. "I must say, Francis has been a brick. Don't know how we managed without Philip. The new man is useless."

"Well, you did a splendid job, Mother," beamed Mr. Knowles, patting her on the back.

Topping had retired to his quarters for a final spit and polish. He ran lightly down his stairs, hair gleaming, looking as if he had stepped out of a bandbox. He glanced around the buffet. "Jolly good show," he called out, sounding like Mr. Nightingale. He flashed his teeth in a wide smile and wafted out, leaving a cloud of perfume behind him.

Solomon nodded his head. "Very good show, oh, thou scented one. Oh my goodness, are these men that they scent themselves like women?"

"Getting soft," rumbled Knowles. "Need another war to stiffen 'em up."

Solomon fingered the rows of medals on his chest. "These I won with real men, proper sahibs. The only scent they carried was good whisky, cigars, gunpowder. Ayee, real sahibs." He clacked his tongue regretfully.

A sound of excited laughter and voices filtered back to them from the reception areas of the front. "Sahib," said Solomon, "is it permitted we see the arrivals?"

"Why not?" said Mr. Knowles.

They stood in a small group, watching the dancers stream in. Handsome men, beautiful women; tonight they were all splendid. All was brilliant with colour and laughter, it was a night to enjoy, to dance until dawn.

Mary, in her midnight blue, backless, down-to-the-floor gown, was escorted by Robert and Andrew. Her eyes sparkled like sapphires.

"Lovely, lovely," sighed Mrs. Knowles. "How beautiful she is."

"Mother, you're going to lose your little girl," said Mr. Knowles, feeling pangs of pride and pain.

"Nonsense," said Mrs. Knowles, "they're far too young. Besides, that young man's got five years' apprenticeship in front of him."

"That young man," said Mr. Knowles, "has a special course arranged so he'll do it all in eighteen months. Don't you know who he and his brother are?"

"No, I don't."

"Sir Ian McIntosh is their father. Their future's all mapped out."

"Well, I never," gasped Mrs. Knowles. This was beyond

her wildest dreams; wait until she told Mrs. Maughan and Mrs. Barhill—proper green they would be. Looking at her lovely daughter, her mind raced, planning, scheming. Spending.

"Look, sahib," said Solomon slyly, "Sergeant-Major sahib. I am not believing my eyes, missie sahib in such a gown."

Sergeant-Major Barhill was splendid in his very best uniform, moustaches bristling, sword swinging, chest thrown out. Mrs. Barhill was on one arm; she had chosen the black and silver and was nodding graciously at all her acquaintances, well aware of the stir her little party was creating.

Jane was in the backless-almost-topless silver sheath, the pleats from her knees swirling, her head held high, face like a flower, eyes luminous like a cat in the dark.

"My God!" said Mrs. Knowles. "I don't believe it! The old bugger's never going to let her get away with that; he's been in the sun too long. She looks ravishing—the men will be all over her."

"What I want to know," said Mrs. Fitter Jones, who had materialized beside her, "is where did they get those frocks, eh? Proper fashion plates they both are. They must have put something in the Sergeant-Major's chota hazri. Can't be himself, isn't it?"

"My heavens!" gasped Mrs. Darsi Jones, who had joined her cronies. "Has that Papworth creature gone out of her mind—what is this, the bazaar?"

"Baba, baba," muttered Solomon, rolling his eyes. Never in his life had he seen such an exhibition.

Vivien Papworth had swept in, leaning on a young officer's arm. On her breasts were round coils of silver metal; a wide pair of shimmering pantaloons draped low over her hips exposed the jewel in her navel. Her hair was dressed with ropes of pearls; kohled eyes peered over a silky yashmak. Her costume was quite authentic.

"Quite disgusting," hissed Mrs. Knowles. "A disgrace she is."

"What's holding up those mess-tins?" asked Mrs. Darsi Jones. "Glued on, are they?"

Vivien stood looking about her. "God," she said to the young officer, "need some dynamite under their arses, this crowd does. Tell them it's fancy-dress, and they turn up in their boring old Sunday school rig-outs."

"Never mind," said the young man, "your parents will steal the show. They've dressed up, haven't they?"

Vivien grinned as she draped herself over the bar. "Ma'll have a fit when she sees this boring shower. She can't bear to stand out in a crowd, and judging from what I've seen of this rabble, she's really going to stand out." She started to laugh. "Babu, I'll have a highball, and give the sahib a pink gin. Give me a cigarette, darling—and keep them coming, Babu."

The Papworths Senior arrived. Mr. Papworth was dressed as a turk, jewelled turban, curly-toed shoes. Mrs. Papworth (Mrs. Barhill whispered unkindly to her bosom-bow, Mrs. Maughan) looked like a Christmas cracker. She was arrayed in the most extraordinary conglomeration of coloured tulle skirts, topped by a headdress of peacock feathers. The Nightingales and the Grundys were hot on their master's heels, in strong competition for unusual costume of the night.

"Crumbs," said Mary, laughing. "This has got to be a mistake. They look like the cabaret—wonder who talked them into it?"

Discreetly stationed at the back of the reception hall, by the bar door, Les Topping felt a glow of satisfaction. He moved to the bar and ordered some gin. "How embarrassing, darling," he muttered to Vivien Papworth. "Your camp does clash rather with the residents."

She blew out a long stream of smoke, then slid off her stool and walked to the door, looking around the assembled crowd. Laughing, she walked back and tossed back her high-ball. "What a scream," she said calmly. "Daddy will have a fit when he realises—take some time, though. He never really looks at the hoi polloi. And the others won't dare tell him."

Topping gritted his teeth and walked out. She had a skin as thick as a rhinoceros.

The Honourable Bertram led his wife onto the dance floor. Happily, they whirled about, pleased with the decorations, delighted with their costumes; not yet aware that they were more or less unique. Gradually the floor filled up, and the ball began.

Mrs. Maughan sat herself in a seat reserved for Mrs. Knowles just outside the bar door, where she could see everything going on in every direction. She fanned herself. Danced non-stop for two hours, she had. Quite worn out, she was, feet sore.

She put her head round the door. "Babu," she called out, "I'll have a port and lemonade with plenty of ice."

"Yes, mem," said Babu. "You fetching, cannot leave counter."

Grumbling, she got up. "Babu," she said, "d'you know whose idea it was to tell the bosses it was fancy dress?"

"No, mem. Papworth missie 'jolly good show,' eh?" He laughed at his joke.

"Don't be cheeky," said Mrs. Maughan, sipping her drink. She stared at a handsome young man whom she vaguely recognised as Mary's beau. He was waiting to be served. "Hello, who are you?"

"Robert McIntosh, ma'am, new apprentice."

"Sweet on Mary Knowles, aren't you?"

"Yes, ma'am." He grinned. Silly old fool—women like her had to know everything.

Acute eyes drilled his. "Nice gel, Mary, no nonsense, mind."

"No, ma'am." Good heavens, who did she think she was?

Mrs. Maughan picked up her glass and turned to leave. Her dangling, lacy sleeve caught on a board tacked to the front of the bar, hidden by the stools. "What's that?" she said as Robert sought to extricate her.

"Some kind of notice, looks like a police notice."

Babu leaned over the bar. "It is police notice; Higgins sahib ordering display murdered woman in reservoir."

"Let's have a look at her," said Mrs. Maughan busily. "Hear her head was cut off, quite indecent."

Robert was staring, puzzled. "But it's her," he said.

Mrs. Maughan's nose twitched. "Who?"

"Blonde woman we travelled with on the train couple of weeks ago. Quite fun she was, really, but not quite—" He broke off.

"Not quite pukka, eh?"

"Well, you know," Robert said. "But it's definitely her. Poor thing," he added, "she had a pretty voice—what a way to go."

"Thought so," said Mrs. Maughan grimly. "Music hall gel—bound to come to a sticky end."

"She said she was coming to join her husband here."

"Husband?" Mrs. Maughan sipped her drink greedily, her eyes avid.

"Papworth, she said. 'Mrs. Bertram Papworth, that's me'—I can hear her now," Robert said. He grinned. "Good memory, what?"

Well, well! Mrs. Maughan wriggled with ecstasy. What a night this promised to be! She returned to her position outside the bar door, but did not sit down. Keenly, her eyes scanned the dancers. Yes, she knew she'd seen him lurking about.

"Yoohoo, Superintendent Higgins," she called. "I have some news for you."

He hadn't come.

Jane stared about her, a numb aching void filling her. She looked so nice, and all for nothing. What did it mean when he wasn't there?

But he hadn't said he would come, had he?

141

\*          \*          \*

In her sea-green gown, Claire floated on the crystal floor in Joseph's arms. Edna was in a back room somewhere, playing poker and swilling gin. What kind of a woman was Edna Edwards anyway?

Claire giggled; better than being a bird, though—or a bicycle.

"What's so funny, my love?" Joseph asked tenderly.

"Nothing," Claire said, lapsing back into depression. Joseph had just asked her to marry him. She should have been deliriously happy, it was what she had yearned for for so long, it would give her unborn child its rightful father. He and Edna were getting a divorce, he had said; he had confessed everything to her.

"Was she upset?" Claire had asked.

"No, she raised her glass and said, 'Here's to health, wealth, and happiness.'"

Claire wished she didn't know that old man Edwards was running around distributing his fortune, giving it all away, cutting his children off without a penny. She wished she didn't think, in her heart of hearts, that it was because Edna was now without prospects that Joseph had finally decided to divorce her. Somehow, it made everything so sordid.

She stood stock still in the middle of the floor while the dancing couples spun around.

Good God, she loved Sonny. She really did. She loved him!

In a swirl of sea-green chiffon, Claire ran from the floor, her eyes searching for Sonny. He was there somewhere. She'd find him. That over-ripe Ray woman could take a jump.

Solomon stood at an open door, getting a breather. The night was hot and still now, when it had started off so promisingly cool.

"Sky most strange color," he said to Mr. Knowles, who joined him, easing his collar. "Is not good, and birds fly around and around, not good. Hawks do not fly at night, sa'b. I am not liking it."

"Think it'll storm?" asked Mr. Knowles anxiously. It would ruin most of the pavillions, and they would have to see about lifting the carpets.

"Not knowing, sahib."

"Well, let's hope it holds off until the dance is over," said Mr. Knowles. "Wireless didn't give us any storm warnings. Soon be morning—or dawn at least—they've all had a good time."

"Very good time, sahib, best time ever," said Solomon. Uri, truly his feet ached. Soon, soon, Chandhi would be stroking him all over, soothing him with sweet oils. Her lips and soft fingers were most delicious. Ayee.

Jane smiled as she walked by them to the terrace at the back of the Institute. Paper lanterns cast a soft glow, a radiant haze. The water in the swimming pool moved back and forth slowly, lazily. Someone must have been swimming. It would be nice to swim, to get out of her mocking clothes, to float and forget.

Her heart was breaking.

She froze at his voice. He walked towards her, white suit, soft hat.

"Jane, Jane, how beautiful you look."

Her heart spun, soared, sang. She sparkled in her silver gown; her eyes grew as luminous as a cat's. Regally, she waited.

"I have a motor—come for a drive with me."

"Where to?"

"Oh! Anywhere. I want to talk to you."

Jane tucked her hand in his arm. "I was expecting you," she said calmly. "We have a lot to talk about, don't we?"

Superintendent Higgins waited until the Paul Jones began, then he approached the alcove where the Papworth party was seated.

"Good evening, sir," he said pleasantly.

Mr. Papworth looked down his nose at him. "What d'ja want, eh? Policeman, what?"

"Yes, sir, Higgins, Superintendent Higgins. We have met before, if you remember. Some Railway business."

"Uh? Oh, yes, yes, well, what d'ja want?" Rude blighter.

"I believe you know this young woman, sir." Higgins held out a photograph.

"Never seen her before in my life."

"That's very odd—because she told several people that she was your wife."

Papworth turned purple. "Nonsense, utter nonsense," he bellowed. Several interested parties close by turned to listen.

"I remember her," Mrs. Papworth said clearly. "Saucy bitch, I threw her out, knew what she was after, money. Females like her invent some kind of blackmailing story. Bloodsuckers. But I stood up to her. In the end she pretended she had made a mistake."

"Well, sir, madam," Higgins said, still very pleasant, "I think we have a lot to talk about, don't we?"

Mrs. Knowles rubbed her temples and looked at her husband. "It's been a long day," she said. "I feel quite dizzy. D'you think it would matter if we left early? We can supervise the clearing up in the morning."

"I think we've put in more than our share," said Mr. Knowles. "Hang on, and I'll have a word with Topping, then we'll leave. Must admit I feel quite dizzy too, must be the heat."

Mrs. Knowles sat down, longing for her bed. Cool white sheets, fan blowing, nice cup of tea.

The conga started, all the dancers crowding to the floor, laughing, still full of energy, spirits still high, determined to dance until daybreak.

"Dear me," said Mrs. Barhill, unable to remember the last time she had enjoyed herself so much. "The conga's too much for me; I'm sitting this one out."

"Speak for yourself," said Mrs. Maughan. "I love a good

romp." She attached herself to Robert's waist and kicked her foot out with great glee. "Life in the old girl yet," she said happily. "One two shake—kick—pom-pom—"

A cloud of balloons cascaded down.

"Lovely, lovely!" cried Mary, in front of Robert. She turned her head and laughed into his eyes. Round and round they spun, the balloons covering the floor, kicking through them like foam on the sea-shore, popping, laughter, spinning, spinning, spinning.

The decorations slid down, entwining them, the crystal floor was dissolving under their flying feet. Mary laughed into Robert's face. "For ever and ever," she cried. "For ever and ever!"

The plaster on the ceiling started to fall down like snow-flakes. Faster and faster. "For ever and ever," Robert cried. They whirled around, giddy, giddy, giddy, snowflakes and balloons and streamers.

For ever and ever, for ever and ever.

On a hill overlooking the town, in a Stutz Bearcat five miles long, pistachio green outside, strawberry pink inside, Jane leaned her head on MacNamara's shoulder and watched the dawn streak the sky. Amazing, the colours were, blood-red, purple, blue. Royal colours.

There were noises in the trees and lush undergrowth, a constant chatter and murmur, like life itself busy with living.

"How strange everything is," Jane whispered. "How grand." She was going to America with MacNamara. The future was a dazzling vista.

Lightning cracked across the hills, jagged streaks that seemed to cut the skies in two. Suddenly there was a huge crack, a great sound.

"Look, look!" Jane cried, sitting up. The angry whiplash cracked and splattered from the great black queen on the crag to the marble white queen in the centre of the town below. Eyeball to eyeball they exchanged glares, electricity shooting through the air between them.

"The black queen, she's winning, she's killing the white queen," Jane whispered, not daring to move.

A great crack, a violent sound, and slowly the marble statue sank from sight. A shudder, and slowly all the town seemed to float down flat upon the surface of the plain; dust and rubble. The music from the Institute hung on the air for a moment, faster and faster, for ever and ever, then gently died away.

There were no church bells on the third Sunday; there was no church. There were no chatting groups of church-goers. The Railway yard and station were quiet. There was no hissing of steam, no whistles. Mrs. Briggs's cocks were quiet; Mrs. Jameson's goats disturbed no one.

There was a slight breeze and, blowing before it, a cluster of gaily-coloured balloons scurried and bounced until they were caught up on a large marble hand pointing to the sky. They twisted and twirled around aimlessly, until the heat of the sun popped them one by one.

There was a town, J.M.P. It was on the Loop Line, but no train stops there now. It was a long time ago.